Journey to an Unknown Planet
Joshua DeVries

I dedicate this book to my loving mom.

Journey to an Unknown Planet

©2015 by Joshua DeVries

Joshua DeVries has asserted his right under the Copyright, Designs and Patent Act, 1988, to be identified as the Author of this work.

Second Edition

Published in the United State of America in 2015.

Chapter 1

3-2-1 Blast-off. I was on my way to the moon. *I hope I can get the food for the 10,000s of people on the moon, I* thought. *If anyone could do it from the University of Space Exploration Class of 2026, it would be me. I, Jackson Robert Williams, was the best pilot in the class of 2026.* I checked my dials. I was about ready to be pulled into the moon's gravity. Suddenly, I heard a beeping noise coming from one of the many screens that surrounded me. I looked at the beeping blue screen. It flashed, "YOU ARE GOING TO MISS THE MOON." I was very frightened. I radioed for help, but the people on the moon were not at the control tower, or if they were they did not acknowledge me. My oxygen levels were very low and I slowly drifted into a coma.

When I came to, I opened my eyes to see a purple sky above me. Giant mushrooms towered like trees. Grass rose 10 feet into the air. Something crawled across my arm. "Ahh!" I screamed. Then I passed out. Again.

When I came to, I was still lying on my back with giant foliage all around me. Suddenly, I froze. I saw a weird bug-like creature crawling across my arm. The bug-like creature looked like a human, because it walked upright, but it was orange and very small. It had an antenna on top of its head which had a leaf on top. I have a phobia of bugs and I was petrified of this little creature. One time in a museum when bugs were on display and the lady let me hold one, I had fainted. The bug like creature started muttering, then bit my arm through my spacesuit! I sat up as I screamed in pain, "Yow!" These Padmin are strong.

I sat as if I was frozen in place. The creature started to speak in its high pitched voice. "Hello, creature from another planet. My name is Womnolhi. Our people are called Padmin. Sorry for biting you. Padmin can sense the danger of something by biting into it. We use our antenna to hit enemies. We can whistle with our antenna, and then the nearest 100 Padmin will come." The Padmin stopped talking and blew his whistle. In about 50 seconds Padmin had gathered around me.

"Help!" I hollered expecting them all to bite me, but instead they were running all over me. While I was in a frozen stupor. I noticed that some of the Padmin had flowers on the top of their heads instead of leaves. The Padmin were also a wide variety of colors.

"How do you know our language?" I nervously asked Womnolhi.

"Well, one day many years ago a human came to our planet. He taught us your language and the new generations have used it ever since."

Someone must have already been here. How did he get off the Padmins' planet? I wondered. Maybe he was still here! Womnolhi went on, "Now this human is sending many creatures against us. We have been endangered for many years."

"Wow," I pronounced. I was a little less nervous about all these creatures. "Well, my name is Jackson and why are all of you different colors? You're like a rainbow of colors!"

"Well, we can explain that. The red Padmin cannot be harmed by fire and are also the best and strongest fighters. Pink means that the Padmin can fly and that they are the engineers. Blue Padmin can go underwater and also work on the farm. The green color represents the ability to work well with trees. I am orange which means that I am the leader."

"So there is water here?" I interrupted.

"Yes there is." Womnolhi continued with his explanation, "Yellow Padmin can't be harmed by electricity. Gray Padmin can break hard objects easily. The flowers on the Padmin's head means that the Padmin is a girl. The leaf means that the Padmin is a boy."

"That's awesome!" I remarked. These insect like creatures looked harmless enough. I felt a little more comfortable around them, now that I knew more about them.

"What type of skin is that?" asked Womnolhi pointing a small finger at my white space suit.

"Oh," I replied as I looked down at my spacesuit. "This isn't my skin. This is my suit. My suit is waterproof. My helmet is also waterproof and it also has microphone so when I talk, everyone can hear my voice as if it wasn't in a helmet. My suit can resist the cold up to negative 100 degrees Celsius and the heat up to 200 degree Celsius. It can survive almost every weather condition. Now I have one favor to ask you guys. Can you help me build my spaceship so that I can get home?" My training had taught me how to repair a broken spacecraft, but I needed more man power.

"Sure," piped up the Padmin, "but then you need to do use a favor. You need to help us defeat all our enemies."

"Ok," I agreed. Little did I know what lay ahead. Thankfully, I had enough food to survive many months because of all the food in my crashed spacecraft. Hopefully it had survived the crash.

I followed Womnolhi as he scurried off down the trail which led into the tall grasses. "How tall is the average Padmin?" I inquired.

"Usually we are about 1 foot tall. We can still know how to get around though, because we have all sorts of trails through the foliage. Hopefully you can fit on the thin trails."

"Yeah," I responded, trying to keep up with him.

"All the Padmin listen to me and do whatever I say. I need to find a whistle for you, though. If you whistle they will all come to your aid as well. Any Padmin who whistles will be helped."

Thankfully I had learned how to whistle from my dad who loves to whistle. "Oh," I exclaimed, "I already know how to whistle." I showed Womnolhi how I whistled. When he heard the noise he leaped into the air.

"That is amazing," he laughed. Suddenly about 100 Padmin burst out of the woods. My heart skipped a beat. Womnolhi told them what had happened, "When he moves his mouth it whistles. You need to come when he calls."

"Ok!" shouted the Padmin. The Padmin quickly darted back into the foliage.

Womnolhi began talking again, "When we battle our enemies you can throw us. We will land on top of the enemies to attack their head and appendages. That's how you can help because you are so tall and strong that you can throw us very far."

We walked for some distance. Giant grasses grew on either side on the trail. Suddenly, we came to a place where many Padmin were cultivating a group of flowers. Womnolhi explained, "These are our farms. We eat these flowers. They provide all the vitamins and minerals that we need." I looked at the flowers. They were all green with a glowing pink cylinder in the middle. The plant was about a half a foot tall. Suddenly one of the blue Padmin saw me and screeched, "Run."

All the Padmin stampeded to get out of the way as I walked towards them. Womnolhi shouted, "Its ok. He is our friend. Go tell your neighbors to be prepared for us."

The Padmin calmed down and left the farms to tell all their friends about me. We continued down the trail. As we walked through the white sand I noticed that all around me that the grasses on either side now had some flower sort of things growing on top of them. Suddenly, a 5 foot tall creature appeared in front of us. Womnolhi screamed, "It's a Golumpet." I'm six foot three inches and even I was scared. The creature had two huge eyes; it had a tongue that licked the ground as it walked. It had no arms. I suddenly realized that Womnolhi was screaming "Pick me up and throw me at the Golumpet. There are lots of these around and most of them are easy to destroy."

I shuddered. I deftly picked up Womnolhi and quickly threw him onto the Golumpet. Womnolhi started hitting the Golumpet with his leaf that was on his antenna. The Golumpet gave a screech and toppled over, then it lay still. Womnolhi panted, "I hit him with my antenna before he could lick me with his tongue. If his tongue licks us we can't get unstuck and the Golumpet promptly swallows us."

Womnolhi asked, "Can you help me bring this Golumpet to our base?"

I picked up the Golumpet by its legs. The creature was not very heavy at all. Womnolhi brought me to a giant clearing. There were thousands of Padmin in one gathering. "This is our base." Womnolhi exclaimed. "I live in that little hole over there in the ground." Womnolhi pointed at a little hill that was all orange and pronounced, "All the Padmin are the same color as their houses."

I watched the Padmin work. I realized that the Padmin were like us in many ways. They had two arms and two legs. The only thing different is that they had huge ears compared to their size, they were colored, and very small. "How is everyone so organized?" I asked Womnolhi as we walked towards a large pathway.

"Oh," replied Womnolhi, "All of the Padmin have little antenna that communicate to each other on what the other Padmin are thinking, which makes our city so organized. The antenna are the same as the antenna that we attack creatures with."

Womnolhi brought me through the large pathway. *What I am going to do with this Golumpet that I am dragging, I* thought. A giant shed loomed up in front of us. The only difference with our sheds on earth was that this shed was sixty feet tall, and it was all built out of wood. Womnolhi enthusiastically exclaimed, "Here it is!"

"Here what is?" I inquired.

"This is our building for storing all our equipment in. We call it 'the Shed'," he responded. I looked around me again. I had no idea how they ever made it with wood. Womnolhi hummed and several Padmin came out of the building cheering because I had killed a Golumpet. They led me to a giant wooded contraption. The machine was all black with brown spots. It had a huge purple tube that was about twelve feet tall. A tube wound around the back and into a funnel. The funnel was pushing a gooey mush into a container which moved on a conveyor belt. The goo would stop flowing till another container was in place. On the side of the machine were three big containers that looked like they had some really weird chemicals in them. The containers were being dropped into a bucket which was being held by some Padmin. The whole contraption was about twenty feet long, ten feet tall, and ten foot wide. Womnolhi announced, "This is our Neutrizer. We put all of the creatures that we kill in here and the machine crushes them into a pulp that we put on our plants. Drop the animal here."

I dropped the animal and 10 Padmin heaved it into the Neutrizer. The machine lurched and then sucked the animal up through the tube. It made a weird gurgling sound and I heard a big crunching noise. I heard some splashing and looked at the back of the Neutrizer. The funnel was pouring the gunk into the containers at a rapid speed. When the funnel turned off there were twelve bottles in the container that the helper was carrying.

Womnolhi hummed again and the Padmin ran to another machine in the Shed. It was very small compared to the Neutrizer. It was only as tall as the Padmin themselves. It had all sorts of antenna sticking out of it. The whole machine was glowing with an eerie sort of green light. There were buttons all over it. It was made out of a weird type of steel. It didn't look like anything that we had on the earth or on the moon. Womnolhi pronounced, "This is the Cantseeum. It is the machine that makes our planet transparent from the eyes and radar of your people. We can see you but you cannot see us. The only thing that you can do is fly out of your planet. We don't have the resources to do that but we don't really care. We would be content with everything that we have, if only there weren't all sorts of creatures that we are afraid of.   There is one called a KillShooter which shoots rocks out of its mouth and digs super deep holes for people to fall into. We will help you defeat that one tomorrow. So far all our tries have ended in failure."

"You want me to fight that thing?" I asked incredulously.

"Yes," Womnolhi replied, "If you can throw us onto the Golumpet, you can easily destroy the KillShooter. The other human defeated a bunch of our enemies before he went insane. Now he has changed the creatures so they destroy us. You need to kill the human then peace will come to our planet. If you kill the evil human then we will help you get off the planet."

Womnolhi brought me to his house. He said, "You can sleep outside tonight. I have ordered some Padmin to construct a giant house for you to sleep in."

"Ok," I agreed. I was amazed. I couldn't believe how organized the Padmin's colony was. *Earth should learn from this,* I thought. The night was cool. I lay on my back and slept very soundly for I had had a very crazy day.

Chapter 2

I woke up with a start. Padmin were scurrying all around. I quickly got up. A huge figure rose up in front of me. It was about ten feet tall. It had the wings of a bat. Its body was hairy and it had two pink glowing eyes. It was picking up Padmin with its skinny feet, tossing them into the air, and then catching them in his mouth. It would swallow one and then do it again. The Padmin could do nothing against the beast except for run into their homes. I would have been more confident if the creature couldn't fly. It flew to my heard and tried to claw my eyes out with its feet! I blew my whistle which calmed the Padmin down. I then started throwing Padmin onto the Flyereater. (Which I later learned it was named).The Padmin held on as the creature flapped its wings. The Padmin valiantly started hitting it with their antenna. Finally, the Flyereater died and slowly drifted down to the ground.

The Padmin were overjoyed. They gathered around the bat creature and picked it up. They brought it to the Shed. Womnolhi hollered, "You just killed the notorious Flyereater. It has terrorized our village for many years. We have no one to throw us at the creatures that terrorize our village. Thank you!"

All the Padmin shouted in unison, "Thank you very much!"

The Padmin that had picked up the Flyereater started walking towards the Shed. Womnolhi hummed and the Neutrizer was pushed out. The machine jerked to life and sucked the Flyereater into it. Twenty jars were quickly filled before the machine shut off. The Padmin that had carried the Flyereater went back to their homes. I went to the ground next to Womnolhi house and lay down to rest.

I must have fallen asleep because I was awakened the next morning by a giant noise that sounded like a giant horn. I sat up. Womnolhi was talking into a giant piece of rock. Womnolhi spoke, "My fellow Padmin. It is now time to find food for our human guest."

"Wait!" I interrupted.

But Womnolhi went on, "Where can we find food?"

All the Padmin started talking at once, "We can feed him creatures like the Golumpets."

"No, those are gross. That's a bad idea."

"No, it isn't."

"Yeah, it is."

Finally, I spoke up and hollered, "I already have food!"

All the havoc stopped instantly. The Padmin stared up at me in wonder. Most of them had never heard me speak before. Womnolhi looked up at me. He spoke into the rock, "Oh, the human already has food."

I don't know why the Padmin call me "the human", because I told them that my name was Jackson. The Padmin were very much in awe of me, because I had defeated the Flyereater. Womnolhi shouted into the rock again, "I have called a council of war. Every Padmin needs to come and stand around the rock."

As soon as the Padmin were around the rock Womnolhi started to speak, "Fellow Padmin. We need to help the human defeat all our enemies. If he does that we will help him build his flying thing."

"Ok!" shouted all the Padmin.

Womnolhi went on, "We are going to attack the Giant Rockshooter today."

"Gasp," said all the Padmin, in unison.

"Everyone needs to prepare, so rest and eat until I call you," stated Womnolhi.

The Padmin filed away and went into their houses or into their fields. Womnolhi stood next to me. He motioned for me to follow him. I did so and he brought me to a giant building and said, "This is your house. You will find a bed inside."

"Thanks," I replied. I was very happy. After a night on the cold ground you should be very thankful for a house, or at least I was. I crawled into the house. It wasn't really a house though. It was all dirt and was 10 feet long, 10 feet wide, but only 3 feet tall. *Oh well,* I thought, *At least I only have to sleep in it.* The floor was actually pretty comfortable. I went to sleep and slept soundly. I dreamed about my family. They were sitting in our living room and they were all crying. In my dream, I could see my, mom, dad, siblings, and even my fiancé Makayla. I woke up with tears on my face, knowing I had to defeat these enemies and get home soon!

The horn awakened me again the next day. *It must be time for the fight,* I thought. *I hope we defeat the Giant Rockshooter.* All the Padmin gathered around the rock once more. Womnolhi started talking, "Now is the time for war. Follow me Padmin."

I followed Womnolhi down a path. The Padmin and I walked for about an hour. Suddenly, in front of us I heard a tremendous roar. All the Padmin ran and hid behind me. I bravely stepped forward. There in a giant pit of sand was the giant Rockshooter. It was a monstrous worm-like creature. In my estimation he was about fifteen feet long and a foot high with pale skin. Its eyes were a bright red. It was monstrous. Its mouth was all purple. The head of the creature looked like a fish's head. Worst of all, it had a mammoth purple, mouth that was shooting rocks at us. The Padmin and I leaped out of the way just as a huge boulder rolled past us. Womnolhi ordered me to throw some Padmin onto the creature. Before it shot a rock it would raise its head of the ground then smash its head back onto the sand to shoot the rock out of its mouth. Then the creature would dive into the ground and open its mouth to suck in some more rocks and sand. The Padmin would also fall into its open mouth when I catapulted them onto the creature. Finally, I couldn't bear to see the Padmin die any longer so I stepped forward. I threw myself onto the creature. I hit the Giant Rockshooter's head but my fist didn't do anything. I was knocked down by a huge boulder that was just leaving its mouth. I revived just as the creature was diving into the dirt to swallow some more sand and rocks. The rock sucking began, and this time nine more Padmin were gobbled up. As the creature rose again, I stepped up to the creature and hit it on the back of its fifteen foot body. Thankfully I could still use my right hand, because my left hand still hurt extremely. The creature gave a tremendous roar, leaped into the air, and lay in the dirt completely still.

The Padmin let out a cheer and rushed forward. We had lost about twenty Padmin. The rest of the Padmin lifted the dead Giant Rockshooter and brought it back to the base. I followed along. I was exhausted. When the Padmin got home they all gathered around me and shouted, "Hail the mighty warrior. Huzzah! Huzzah!"

"That human is strong!" shouted one Padmin.

"He defeated the creature that ate my friend Egoli!" yelled a jumping blue Padmin.

"Hurray for the human!" shouted all the Padmin at once.

Later that night Womnolhi took me to the Shed. There were about one hundred cans stacked inside along the wall of the Shed. With a sweep of his arm Womnolhi pronounced, "This is all the flower food that the Giant Rockshooter gave us. Thank you for defeating him."

"You're welcome," I replied. We waked down the path that led to the Padmin's village. Just as Womnolhi began explaining to me a little about the enemies that were left to fight, a giant shadow had passed over us. I looked up and saw what appeared to be a spider, but it only had four stick-like legs. Its legs were connected to a body that was covered in really long hair. The creature was about fifteen feet tall. The body was three feet in circumference. It looked extremely ugly. It was walking around and stepping on the Padmin that were running around. The creature was trying to crush the Padmin which were wildly trying to get to shelter. Womnolhi was screaming, "Blow your whistle, human. This is one of the enemies I was talking about. It's the Spiwalker!"

I obeyed and all the Padmin calmly gathered around me. Womnolhi instructed me, "Pick up the red Padmin and hurl them onto the Spiwalker. The red are the best fighters so hurry."

I threw the red Padmin at the Spiwalker. They landed on the hair of the Spiwalker and started hitting the creature with their antenna. I tried throwing some gray Padmin at the creature's legs. The legs crumbled at the weight of the gray Padmin, because the gray Padmin were extra heavy. The creature was shaking its body which caused the red Padmin to lose their hold on the Spiwalker's head and fly off the creature into the grass. Every time the Padmin fell off the Spiwalker I would whistle and they would come back to me. Finally, the Spiwalker collapsed to the ground, dead and defeated. The Padmin had a hard time bringing the Spiwalker to the Neutrizer but they managed to do it. The sky darkened, it was the end of the day. I went to my home and slept soundly.

Chapter 3

I woke up later the nest day. The Padmin were doing their normal chores. I visited the farms to see if I could help. One of the blue Padmin that worked at the farm showed me a very small pile of jars which were full of flower food. They had made a cart for me to push the jars around the fields so that they could sprinkle the flower food onto the flowers. The Padmin were very smart inventors. They only used wood. I asked Womnolhi, "Where did you get the wood to build this cart from?"

"The green Padmin get the wood from the forest that is grown in the mountains north of here. Tomorrow we will go get more wood. Our supplies are very low after building your house."

I need supplies, too, I thought. *I need human food.* I told Womnolhi, "I am going back to my spacecraft to collect what is left of my food."

"Ok," Womnolhi warned, "but be careful where you go."

I took the cart and walked down the path that Womnolhi and I had walked on only a few days ago. I came to where my space craft had crashed. Nothing was there except the food, and it had been thrown around. *Who did this?* I thought. *And why did they take everything, but leave the food. Maybe it was that creature last night.* Suddenly I became scared. I quickly put all the food in my cart and hurried home.

I ran back to the village so fast that by the time I had arrived I was famished. I had hardly eaten in the last few days. I ate a whole can of ice-cream and then a hamburger. Five years ago all the food that went into space had to be dehydrated. Thankfully, a man named Jon VanGeissen had invented a container that somehow kept the food eatable without having to dehydrate it. I felt sick. After that I lay down in my home and took a short nap.

I woke up suddenly. Womnolhi was standing by me. He spoke, "I am going to show you how our Padmin are born. Follow me. We are going to the Padplant Palace."

"Ok," I yawned as I got up and followed Womnolhi. We walked past the Shed. Womnolhi led me to a building. The building was shaped like a half a bubble. It was made out of pure glass. "How do you make this stuff?" I inquired as I touched the outside of the building.

"Oh that's Ceethrough. Our engineers make it. We heat up sand. It's easy," replied Womnolhi.

We entered the building. Inside there were a lot of yellow Padmin. They were spreading water on all the tiny plants that were in the ground. Womnolhi picked up a grey plant and up popped a rock Padmin. I was shocked. "Yikes," I yelled, "how did you do that?"

"Oh," replied Womnolhi, "those plants are Padplants." I looked around the Padplant Palace. There were at least one thousand Padplants. Womnolhi went on, "We can know if the Padmin is ready to be pulled by the flower or leaf that is on top of their antenna. When the leaf or flower is completely grown then we pick the Padmin. We water and provide sunlight for the Padplants so they turn into strong Padmin. You can tell which color the Padmin is going to be by the color of the stem of each plant. There are no young Padmin, because Padmin are born as adults."

"Oh," I yawned. "I was wondering why I hadn't noticed any children. But, isn't it sad without children?"

"No, we didn't even know what young was until the last human came and tried to explain. Why would we want smaller versions of ourselves when we can just have big ones to start?"

He had a good point. All this talk of children, though, was making me miss my family. "I am going to my house, Womnolhi," I told him. "I really miss my family. I hope that we defeat all of the giants soon! I am going back to my house to sleep. Goodbye." Womnolhi waved and I walked back to my house ate ten chicken nuggets and went to sleep.

The next morning I went to Womnolhi's house. He told me that we were going to walk for about two hours so I had brought two sub sandwiches from the stock of food that I had, just in case I got hungry. For some reason, I wasn't as hungry here on the Padmins' planet than on Earth. Maybe it had to do with the climate or something. I love Subway sandwiches with mayo, olives, pickles, French bread, honey mustard, provolone cheese, ham, and lettuce. I had also brought the cart in case we needed it. I followed Womnolhi down a path.

After walking for several miles we walked into a huge clearing. I looked around me. There were all sorts of purple tree-like objects. I went to the side of the path and touched them. They weren't even trees at all. They felt like mushrooms. I looked up and saw that the tops looked like mushrooms also. I asked Womnolhi, "Is this how you build your houses?"

"Yes," replied Womnolhi, "we use the things that you are touching. Those are what we call trees."

So my house is made out of this stuff, I thought. And so are some of the other huts that the Padmin build, other than the dirt Shed that is. Womnolhi spoke again, "The other human said that the trees on our planet are stronger than the trees on your planet."

Yes, I could see he was right. Hundreds of green Padmin were scurrying about the clearing carrying sections of the "trees" all around. They were bringing them to a long, narrow building. I followed Womnolhi towards the building. It was only four feet tall, so I had to bend down to peer inside. It was full of a variety of machinery. There was a machine that looked like a mouth. It was opening and closing very rapidly. A conveyor belt was pushing trees into it. Once the trees were crushed in the mouth-like machine, they would become a pulp-like substance which would flow out of the back of the machine and into a big vat. A second conveyor belt was pushing trees into a machine that compressed them into thin sheets. A third conveyor belt pushed trees into a machine that was making boards out of the trees. It looked like a sawmill back on the earth except for it was on a much smaller scale and the machines were different. I looked at the other side of the building where I saw a pile of metal. Womnolhi followed my gaze and said, "That's our pile of fobulet. It is our only type of metal that we have. We use it to cut trees. We use fobulet to build all of our machinery. It is essential to our living. Some Padmin are mining it out of the mountain. We will go see them next, so you can experience out mining process."

"Ok," I replied as I followed Womnolhi down a nearby path. We walked for about five minutes until we reached a giant electric gate which loomed in front of us. The gate had two enormous posts on either side and 5 electric bars that ran between the two posts. On top of both the posts there was a blinking light. Womnolhi hollered and the gate swung open. We strode past the gate and I saw the mining mountain. Gray

Padmin were pushing little carts around. Womnolhi exclaimed, "As I told you, earlier, the grey Padmin can break rocks, so naturally this is where they work. The mines are big enough for you to go into so follow me."

I followed Womnolhi into an elevator, but I had to crawl because of my great height compared to that of the Padmin. Fortunately, the doors were very large for the massive amounts of fobulet that was transported on it. Thankfully the elevator had no sides--it was just a platform, so I could easily fit on it. I was a bit scared. We were lowered deep underground, past many rocks with fobulet wedged around and between them. The elevator stopped with a clank at the bottom of the mine. The air felt damp and thick. It was hard to breathe. I was still scrunched down in an awkward position because of my height. I sat so I would feel more comfortable and watched the grey Padmin scurrying around. The color of the grey Padmin was so close to that of the fobulet that they blended in almost perfectly. I asked Womnolhi, "Why are the rock Padmin the same color as the fobulet?"

"Well," replied Womnolhi. "That is just how they were born. They were tough and durable, so when we started to mine for fobulet we choose them to mine. As you can see they are very good at their job.

I was amazed. As my eyes adjusted to the darkness I saw hundreds of rock Padmin throwing themselves onto the walls of the mine. The cavern was so ginormous that the sides looked like they were off in the horizon. Amazingly the ceiling of the cave was about fifty feet into the air. I couldn't see any of the sides. I just saw glowing plants protruding out of the rocks all around the cavern. There were glowing plants all around the cavern. There were ledges in the rock that the Padmin were standing on as they broke off chunks of fobulet. The fobulet around them reflected light, which made the walls sparkle. I saw a rock Padmin breaking off a chunk of fobulet and another rock Padmin with a cart on the ledge under him. The piece of broken fobulet would fall into the cart. If the fobulet hit the Padmin carrying the cart then the fobulet would just bounce off him or her, without hurting the Padmin! I then realized that the first ledge had mining Padmin. The next ledge had a cart carrying Padmin and above him was the fobulet-breaking Padmin. I realized that the Padmin were very organized and very industrious little creatures even here down in the mine.

"Let's follow a Padmin with a full cart," Womnolhi instructed. *Easy for him to say,* I thought. *He doesn't have to get out of this elevator.* I struggled out of the cart and followed along behind him trying to not step on any carts or Padmin. In the far corner of the cave there was a conveyor belt which dropped the fobulet into a gapping pit. "That pit has lava under it," Womnolhi explained. "The lava makes the fobulet melt. The melted fobulet is called fore. On a level below us, the fore is poured out into a machine, which molds the fore into whatever we are making at the time. If you want an antenna for a machine, then the molding machine will pour the fobulet into an antenna mold. When the antenna is finished a Padmin takes the antenna out of the mold. Then they cart the antenna to whoever needs it."

"Wow, that's quite a process," I exclaimed. "I need one. Will they make one for me? I could use an extra antenna for the new soundless program that I have been working on in my spare time."

"Sure, I will have it at your house by tomorrow," Womnolhi replied as we strolled back to the elevator. Once we were both on the cart Womnolhi pulled a little rope. The elevator slowly rose again. "What does that rope do?" I asked Womnolhi.

"That rope signals for the four red Padmin who then start pulling the rope that is raising the elevator," continued Womnolhi. "The flying Padmin are engineer Padmin. They made a pulley system so that it will only take four red Padmin to raise or lower this platform."

The elevator came to a stop at the top of the shaft. Womnolhi and I walked off of the elevator platform. Suddenly, I heard a ferocious and loud roar echoing and bouncing off of the sides of the mountain. I immediately whistled. All the rock Padmin that were around my general area, rushed to stand near me. We heard a sound of crunching metal in front of us. Coming up the path was one of the scariest creatures I had ever seen. It was all covered in a glass like substance. It looked like a rhino on steroids that had made it bigger and deadlier. It was about the size of a four school buses. It had horns surrounding its body. Its face looked like a Rottweiler's face. It had two glowing green eyes that made my heart skip a beat. It had no arms, but it had four legs. It came so close that the ground shuddered. I started throwing Padmin onto the creature at about 102 miles per hour. *Thankfully, I was the leading pitcher of the Wyoming Brown Socks for many years,* I thought. (We actually won the Word Series in 2022.) When I threw the rock Padmin the impact of their hard bodies caused all the spikes to break and then the grey Padmin would bounce off and fall to the ground. The creature was running in circles eating Padmin with its short beak. It was also crushing them with its oversized feet. Finally one of the Padmin that I threw landed on the head of the creature. The creature gave a huge moan and flopped onto its side. Then it got back up and started running towards me. I frantically threw the remaining Padmin at the head of the insane creature. The skull of the creature cracked in half and goo started flowing out of it. The Padmin dove out of the way as the huge beast flopped to the ground.

When the Padmin saw that the creature was dead they flocked around me and cheered. "What.....was.......that?" I panted.

Womnolhi shouted over the cheering, "That was the evil thedoput. The thedoput live in the north above the mountains and don't visit here very often. But when they do, they feed on Padmin. We won't bring him back to the Neutrizer, because the thedoput is hazardous to eat. Don't touch that goo or you will become thedoput too. A few years ago, several Padmin touched the goo and they turned into thedoputs right before our eyes, so don't touch it."

After the Padmin had stopped cheering Womnolhi told them to have ten of them follow me around. Then all of us walked down to the tree chopping place. The gate was completely crushed.

I realized that the thedoput had crushed it. I was surprised that the electricity hadn't stopped him. Maybe some creatures are resistant to electric. "Who invented electricity?" I asked Womnolhi.

"As I said before," replied Womnolhi, "the pink Padmin are engineers. They invented electricity with the help of the other human."

We walked back to the tree chopping place. My cart was filled with trees. Womnolhi told ten of the green Padmin to follow him. They obeyed and I pushed the cart back to the village. I was really hungry so I ate my subway sandwiches. Womnolhi complained, "Why are you taking so long we need to hurry? We need to get back to the village and get you ten of every color of Padmin."

"Ok," I replied. We hurried back to the village. When we got back I brought the cart and left it at the shed. Then I went back to my hut that was next to Womnolhi's hut and went to sleep.

Chapter 4

The next morning I woke up to the sound of Padmin standing at my front door. I realized that there was ten of every color. I tried conversing with them. Each color had one leader. Womnolhi walked up and exclaimed, "You can call the blue leader, Blue Leader, and you can call the green leader, Green Leader, and so on."

"Ok," I said.

"I am going to work at the farm again today. You can rest," I told the Padmin.

"We can't," one of the Padmin piped up, "Womnolhi ordered us to always stay by you. We don't mind. It's our job to protect you. We protected the other human, at least until he turned evil, and we will guard you, too."

"Yeah," all the Padmin spoke in unison.

"Oh, well. I guess you can follow me then." I replied. I was in no mood to argue.

I had stored my food in the little space that I had in my house. I took a Cinnamon Toast Crunch box out of the pile of food and ate some. It was really good. I had no bowl so I ate it without milk. The Padmin watched me. I felt bad, so I offered a piece of my cereal to each of them. They took it and ate it. Instantly, they held up their paws for more. I gave them all that I had in my hands. They were really happy with their taste of human food. They bounced along the pathway that led to the Shed. I pushed the Shed doors open and grabbed my cart. I ran to the farm and reported to the farm building, but I couldn't step inside, because I was too big. The blue Padmin that was in charge of the farm came to me. He spoke up, "We don't have any work that can be done by you. Thanks for asking though. Why don't you go see if you can help in the laboratory?"

"Where is the laboratory?" I asked.

Pink Leader motioned for me to follow her. She flew off in the opposite direction of the mountains. The other Padmin and I followed along the ground. She buzzed down a path, then stopped in front of an electric gate and squeaked, "The pink Padmin can fly over the gate, but you need to use the yellow Padmin to destroy it. The evil human built it to harm us."

"Throw us at the gate," interrupted Yellow Leader. I did so and the yellow Padmin held onto the rings of the electric gate and smashed it down. The Padmin and I moved on along the path. The path had a dirt-like material on the ground. It was a lot like the path that I had taken when I first got on the planet. The only difference was that the path had mountains on either side and it was much wider. "Why is the path bigger than the other paths that I have traveled on in other places?" I inquired.

Pink Leader replied, "The path is this wide so that the big equipment that we build has room to get down to the Shed. The pink Padmin build machines like the Neutrizer and the Cantseeum."

Suddenly, I saw a giant creature appear on the path in front of us. It looked like an upright, moving cone that was on fire! It was about ten feet tall. The diameter of the creature was about 8 feet. It was slithering towards us. It had no head but part of the cone was opening and closing to form a mouth. The body was orange and black stripes going around it. The creature was on fire, but the fire wasn't even singing the creature. Where ever the creature went there was a stream of fire following closely behind.

"Throw us at the Quire!" screamed Red Leader. I picked up the red Padmin and started throwing them at the creature. The Padmin landed on the Quire and started hitting the creature with their antenna. Suddenly the creature swirled into a little ball and the fire stopped. The red Padmin ran back to me. "The Quire," panted Red Leader, "It's dead!"

After that slight excitement that I was becoming quite accustomed to, we continued walking down the path that led to the laboratory. We arrived at the laboratory about an hour after we had attacked the Quire. The building was really spacious. It was in a clearing that was surrounded by electric walls. The building was one thousand foot square and seven feet high. I stepped inside. As soon as I stepped inside I was astounded with the amount of machinery my eyes were seeing. There was machinery all around the building. I walked around the building. "Can you give me a tour of the building?" I asked Pink Leader.

"Sure. I would be happy to," he cheerfully replied. He motioned for me to follow him. He led me to an immense machine. It had glowing lights all around it. "This is the fobulet crusher," Pink Leader announced. "The fobulet is crushed into very small pieces so it is easy to melt. Over there is the machine that heats up the fobulet so it turns into liquid." I looked at the other machine. I realized that all the machines were connected by conveyor belts to form a continuous assembly line. Padmin were bringing little carts full if fobulet and dumping them into the machine. Pink Leader pointed and described the other machines to me in order.

"After the machine that heats the fobulet is the machine that divides the liquid fobulet into three different machines," continued Pink Leader. "The first machine makes the fobulet into sheets that are used in other machines. The second machine takes the fobulet and mixes it with trees to make extraordinary strong glue. The third machine makes anything you want. You just put a mold into the machine and that shape will come out. As he describe that machine, I thought about my family back home, and tried to imagine about all the ways such a machine would be handy to us I would have to find out more about it. All the three machines have bins at the end of them," the Pink leader was saying, as I came out of my daydream. "The finished product of the machines drop into the bins and then a Padmin comes. The Padmin take the product out of the container and packages it on the tables that take up the middle of the building. On the other side are the machines for making ceethrough."

"Ceethrough?" I responded.

"Yes," replied the Pink Leader. "I think you people on earth call ceethrough glass."

The Pink Leader was interrupted by laughs from all the other Padmin bodyguards. The Pink Padmin went on, "They think the word glass is funny. Ceethrough is much stronger than glass."

"Wow, that's amazing!" I responded. Arriving back at out village, we ate a hardy supper and settled down to sleep. I woke up with a start in the middle of the night. A creature was visiting us again. I wondered what that creature was doing this time. I could see the golden feet glowing in the moonlight, I stealthily got up and checked the door. After making sure it was bolted, I went back to bed, pulled the covers over my head, and waited for morning.

I must have fallen asleep at one point, because I woke up to the sound of my body guards. They were busy chattering to themselves right outside my door. I had requested Womnolhi to send me extra body guards and Womnolhi had sent ten more Padmin of every color. Now I had twenty Padmin of every color and they were all chattering, a very pleasant sound to wake up to. I went outside to greet them. "What are you talking about?" I yawned.

"The Goldtromper! Didn't you see him? That is what the human turned into when he went insane. The human turned into the Goldtromper, because the Padmin's food didn't react well with the human's digestive system and caused his DNA to mutate! This caused natural growth and different powers. As time went on, these symptoms got worse. It is as tall as that tree!" Yellow Leader pointed at a fifteen foot tall tree. Yellow Leader went on, "The Goldtromper is the scariest of all the enemies. The human is a shade of gold and it has two tiny feet. It sends lightening, water, fire, and rocks. It is extremely hard to fight. One time it came into our village at night and ate three Padmin that had left their houses. That is why we stay in our houses at night."

"Wow," I exclaimed. I never said very much, but I was thinking that in the future I would avoid sampling Padmin food. The last things I needed was to mutate and never see my family again! To never even *be* human! I shuttered

"What is it like on earth?" one of the rock Padmin drew me back from my thoughts.

"Well, almost everyone is a little shorter than me," I answered slowly. "We have different types of trees. We have huts that are much taller than your trees. We have things that let us fly." I laughed. That wasn't a very good description of earth at all.

"Wow," Red Leader breathed.

"Ooooo," ooed one of the Padmin.

The rest of the Padmin looked on in awe. "Did you have any things like us?" asked the White Padmin.

"Yes," I replied. "We have these things called bugs that just crawl or fly around. You look like a bigger version of them plus you guys are way smarter than those insects."

"Hey I'm a girl not a guy!" shouted Pink Leader.

"Me, too," piped up Grey Leader and about twenty other Padmin.

"Oh, sorry," I replied. "You are kinder than them, too," I added to my apology, hoping it would make up for offending them.

We walked into a big field at the end was a mammoth cave. The cave looked like the mouth of a tremendous animal. I love adventures, so I walked to the cave and stepped inside. The Padmin followed me, but they chattered nervously. That should have been my first clue to stop going inside, but my curiosity had gotten the best of me. We walked into the cave for about twenty feet. Suddenly, I smelled an odor that made me quiver. It was putrid. In front of us, slithering down the cave came a colossal worm shooting out the obnoxious smell. It looked about thirty feet long and eight feet around. It looked like a worm, too. I blew my whistle to call the Padmin. We rushed out of the cave before the worm could get us, but we could not out run the worm! The worm curled around the field and closed in on us. I couldn't believe my eyes. It looked like an advancing wall of worm. Like a tunnel that subway trains go through! I started throwing the Padmin at it whit whatever color I could grab! I even threw the red Padmin.

Finally, I only had pink Padmin left around me to throw. I threw them with all my might. I whistled for all the other Padmin and they got into a group behind me. The white Padmin flew to the creatures head and lifted it up then dropped it. The worm slithered which crushed some of my Padmin. Then the worm curled into a ball and lay still. The Padmin and I picked heaved with all our strength together and dragged it towards the Shed. It felt all slimy. It made the walk back to the Shed very hard! Finally we made it and added the worm in the Neutrizer. Thirty jars of flower food came out of the machine. The Padmin and I helped stack the jars in the Shed. Then we went to Womnolhi. "Ten of my Padmin died today," I sadly said.

"Oh, I'm so sorry!" Womnolhi loved his creatures. He wept. "I feel really bad about those Padmin. I will give you more Padmin though."

I was tired, but I still went to ask at the farm to see if they needed help before taking a rest. The same blue Padmin met me and exclaimed, "We do need help now! Can you run some flower food to the north side of the field? Take this new cart and hurry."

I grabbed the cart and rushed to the north side of the field. I knew better then to ask what I needed to hurry. I remembered that the field was about five football fields long, which is a very long way for a tired human to run! The flowers were all about three feet tall. The Padmin had to use ladders to sprinkle flower food onto the middle of the flower; for me it was easy. I delivered the flower food and sat back to admire a job well done. "How do you know when to pick the flowers?" I asked one if the workers.

"Well," he answered. "The middle of the flower is called the glowma. When the glowma glows then we pick the glowma. We send the glowma to a building that makes the glowma into liquid or into chunks for us to eat. It is really delicious. We also can grind glowma with fobulet to make a super strong substance called glowulet. Glowulet is what makes our planet invisible. When we throw it into the air, it fills up the atmosphere to hide us."

34

Glowulet sounded pretty cool. Definitely something I would like to take home with me. "Is there anything that I can do to help you?" I asked.

"Yeah, you could help us by sprinkling a little bit of flower food on all the flowers."

"Ok. Everyone get behind me!" I exclaimed. Everyone did and I picked up a handful of flower food. I threw it into the air. It landed on the flowers. All the Padmin cheered. They lay down on the soft ground and one of them shouted, "Do it to the whole field!"

I did what they asked. Every time I threw a handful they would cheer. I managed to do the whole field in about an hour. Finally I panted, "Thanks for showing me how to do this. I am going to go home now. A least what I considered home to be for now."

"Ok," yelled all the Padmin, "Thank you and see you tomorrow." I went back to my house and devoured a whole bunch of food. I was really hungry, because I hadn't even had time for lunch that day. *Good thing I got all the food from my spaceship that was there*, I thought. *But how much longer will it last? As I settled down to sleep, I mentally calculated how many days of food I had left. One month, maybe two. Then what?*

Chapter 5

The next morning I woke up and ate Cinnamon Toast Crunch for breakfast again. I gave some to the Padmin and they were tremendously happy. I decided I wanted to work in the mines again and headed there to offer my assistance. I moved rocks all around in the cavern. Because I could carry so much, I could save the Padmin about five trips. They were all astatic. It was a blissful feeling to be able to help them so much. As a boy, I had always liked to go into caves. My dad had worked in the Mammoth Cave National Park and he often took me into the caves with him. Thinking about my dad reminded me of my mom. She was a really good cook. Her mashed potatoes were mouthwatering and I used to pretend that the potatoes were mountains. I would even build little caves into them. Then I would pretend that my rice was soldiers that were going into the mountains. It was really fun. How were my parents now? Did they worry about me? With a sigh I realized I had been day dreaming and went back to my work. I worked in the mines for the whole day.

I woke up early the next day and the first thing I did was look at the marks on my wall in the dim light. I had made a small mark for each dat. How many had it been already? Seven-teen days? My poor family! As I continued to think of them, I could hear Womnolhi speaking by the rock, "Everyone who is able to fight come gather around the rock. Today we will fight the Rockcabock. As you all know this creature has been killing our Padmin as they travel home from working in the mines all day. I need everyone to follow the human. I will show him the cave that the Rockcabock lives in. Everyone follow the human! Once he kills all our enemies, we will help him get home!"

All the Padmin rushed to get behind me. I followed Womnolhi down the path that led to the mines, knowing that each enemy I killed would be one creature closer to my voyage home. We walked past the tree chopping clearing. We veered to the left and entered a path. The path was as wide as the path that led to the mines. *I wonder how I hadn't seen this path when I first went to the mines,* I thought. We walked for about four minutes through a canyon. There was green foliage and ferns clung to the sides of the cliffs. Giant trees over shadowed the path. We rounded a corner and there was the mouth of a giant cave. As we walked in my eyes adjusted to the darkness and I noticed that we were in a huge cavern. The walls were thirty feet high. The floor covered one hundred square feet. Little glowing plants were all around the sides of the cavern. I realized a giant lump on the side of the cave. Looking closer, I could see the lump moving. I almost had a heart attack as I leaped back. I squinted and tried to get a better view of the creature. "Is this the creature?" I whispered to Womnolhi. He nodded yes and I looked at the giant caterpillar who appeared to have a shield a glass encasing his back. It was all blue except the creature's back which was all clear. The Rockcabock had two giant pinchers that were opening and closing very rapidly. It rushed at us with its snapping pinchers! I leaped to the side. About ten Padmin were struggling and appeared to be trapped in the claws of the Rockcabock. The creature would use his pinchers to shove Padmin into its mouth. I started throwing Padmin onto the creature's feet to try to cripple him. Padmin were running around and screaming hysterically. The Rockcabock just shook the Padmin off and crushed many of them to death. I realized that the rock Padmin could break the glass substance which was on the creature's back. Those were the Padmin that I needed to throw! I quickly threw twenty rock Padmin onto the creature. The glass on its head shattered! I threw a bunch of red Padmin onto the fractured skull. Suddenly, the Rockcabock reared up to a height of 8 feet and screeched. It slammed its head onto the ground which crushed several Padmin to death. Then the Rockcabock started slithering around the cavern. It would run up the wall and hang onto the ceiling. Then it would let go and fall to the floor. I continually whistled to calm the Padmin down.

As I whistled, I continued in throwing rock Padmin onto the fractured skull of the Rockcabock. The Padmin started whacking the head with their antenna. The creature finally collapsed with exhaustion. It coughed out a huge number of Padmin appendages. Then it lay still.

"Yay!" shouted all the Padmin as they rushed forward to pick up the Rockcabock. The Padmin and I carried the creature back the village and were met with a hardy cheer by the other Padmin. Carrying the heavy body of the Rockcabock made the return was about twice as long. About fifty Padmin had died which was sad, but the Padmin were relieved that the evil tyrant was killed. We put the Rockcabock into the Neutrizer. The machine made a whirling sound and fifty-five jars of flower food were filled. I went back to my house. I was exhausted. That night I slept like a log.

On Day number 18, I woke up when the sun was straight up in the sky. The sun was much closer to this planet so the planet was really humid. It rained for the first time since I had gotten here. The droplets were about a six inches long. *I wonder what makes the rain different than ours?* I thought. I went to the Padplant house to help them. The ceethrough was slid back so the rain could fall on the Padplants. I was really chilled so I decided that today was not a good day to work. I remembered the days when my brother and two sisters and I would jump on the trampoline in the rain. Then we would jump in the hot tub, which would feel really good. I felt like jumping into a hot tub right now, but that wasn't possible clearly. I missed my siblings. I was ready to go home! Next time I saw Womnolhi I would ask him how many enemies were left. In the meantime, even if it wasn't a good day to work at least it would help pass the time.

I decided that it would be a good day to go to the laboratory. "I am going to the laboratory," I called to my bodyguards. "Follow me if you want."

"Ok," they all replied, "Womnolhi ordered us to stick by you through short and tall."

I walked down the path that led to the laboratory. Arriving at the clearing that the laboratory was in, I walked in. I saw a pink Padmin that looked like he was in charge. "How can I help?" I asked.

"Well," he replied. "You and your bodyguards can bring the sheets of fobulet to the work tables."

I did that for the rest of the day. It was really boring, but I still managed to get the job done. Towards the end of the day the Padmin and I went back to the village and sat around sharing stories of our worlds before retiring for the night.

The next morning I woke up to the sound of my Padmin scurrying around my sleeping body. They seemed to be watching me sleep. I got up and had twelve handfuls of my remaining cinnamon toast crunch stash. I gave each Padmin one piece of my cereal. They were really happy. They started chattering amongst themselves. I listened in.

"Did you see the Goldtromper last night?" one blue Padmin excitedly exclaimed.

The green Padmin jumped up and down, "Yeah, it went up to our human's house."

"I know. I saw it look inside to see our human."

"You know that the Goldtromper is really the insane human that taught us his language," I overheard them say. *What!?* I thought and started listening closer.

"Yeah, Womnolhi told me that."

"Did you see the evil human come to my door?" I interrupted.

"Yeah," replied an energetic red Padmin, looking to see how I would react.

Wow, I thought. *I wonder what the insane human was doing at my house. Maybe he is trying to destroy me before I destroy him. I hope he never comes back.* Womnolhi walked over to me and exclaimed, "Can go exploring today? We need to know where the evil human turned Goldtromper is. Don't take any of your Padmin. Be completely silent."

"Ok," I whispered, deciding that while we were out seeking I could ask Womnolhi the questions that had been haunting me about my return home.

"Here, take this PadPad. Where ever you go it moves with you," Womnolhi's voice interrupted my thoughts. "If you run your finger across it you can see where you are going. Our engineers made it as a thank you for all the help that you gave them. You can also call us with this button."

I tried scrolling my finger across the screen. It was like a GPS except that it even showed little details like flowers. It looked so real that it seemed that you were looking at the flowers in real life. I would have asked Womnolhi how the PadPad got its data, but now I needed to hurry. I went back to my base and packed two canned tuna sandwiches. Thankfully, I had my tracker suit and put it on so that my position could be traced as I pursued the Goldtromper.

I went back to Womnolhi and gave him the other end of my tracking device. He took it and walked into the Shed. After he showed me the route we would each take, I gave him one of my DeVries Masks to wear. I showed him how to file away information. Basically, when I say "file" into my mask then the mask saves all that was said in the last ten minutes. These masks had been in use since 2023, when an inventor named Joshua DeVries had come up with the technology and ideas behind it. I remember the day when Mr. DeVries had spoken at an assembly at the University of Space Exploration. Mr. DeVries called me up to help him assemble a satellite using bunny slippers, duct tape, and tinfoil. Mr. DeVries is a really smart guy. My day-dream was interrupted as I approached the river where I was to start searching for the Goldtromper. I put on Mr. DeVries' mask which not only filed information, but also was waterproof and soundproof. I walked into the foliage that was around the shed. I looked at the PadPad. I hit one of the buttons that was on the side of my mask. I had turned on noise canceling mechanism. I looked at the PadPad. It looked like an IPad. It was the same size. It was green and brown and had a giant protective case around it. I went on walking until I came to a river. The river was only twenty feet wide. I saw a lily pad float past me. Suddenly something on the plant moved. I looked again and two Padmin were on the lily pad. They probably didn't realize me because I was noiseless. I heard the talking to each other.

"So Blambet, when are you going to kill Womnolhi?"

"Stop bugging me Gant. I'll do it tomorrow night, when we destroy the Padmin village."

They floated on down the river. I whispered "file" into my mask so that the information would be saved. I must get the news to Womnolhi before tomorrow, but I wanted to focus on the task at hand. It looked as if the village would be in big trouble! I stepped into the river. I slid all the way to the bottom of the river. Thankfully my suit and mask were waterproof, because the river was about ten feet deep. The walls were straight up so there was no way to get out. I decided just to go up the river and look for a way out of the river there. Suddenly, a giant swimming eel knocked me down. I got up onto my feet again. Just then another creature hit my legs. I heard a zap and my legs shook. Thankfully I had my suit on, because clearly I was being bullied by shocking eels and my suit took most of the shock. I nervously walked up the river once more. I stayed along the side wall and watched. I saw weird creatures swim by. One looked like a really unique frog. It had no head and only had two eyes on its body. It had four legs and was all yellow except for the top of the body which was a clear green. There were giant slug like creatures that were like pale pink. They had two eyes that were on antenna that stuck two inches off their heads. It had a giant slimy back that was brushing up sand everywhere blinding me in a watery sandstorm. I wandered into the middle of the stream and was knocked down again. What a job! I was feeling exhausted after just an hour of Goldtromper searching!

I was knocked around by all of the swimming creatures for another thirty minutes. Finally, I managed to get to the side of the stream again. I was so thankful that my suit also had a machine that acted like the gills of a fish enabling me to sleep and breathe underwater. I had a gigantic headache from being knocked around by all those creatures. I fell asleep on the floor of the riverbed and dreamed about my family.

Chapter 6

I woke up in the morning. Sun was streaming through the water. When you get goggles on and swim to the bottom of a pool and look up into the sun there are pillars of light. That is what it looked like. It was beautiful. Then I remembered what my mission was today. I needed to find the base of the evil human turned Goldtromper so I could come back and kill it. I really didn't feel good about killing, even if it had changed into a new creature. I wonder what he thinks about me being here. Does he still think? I walked up the river once again. After walking for about an hour I saw that the sides of the stream weren't as narrow. Now the river was about thirty feet across. I continued to walk until I finally found a spot where the river was so shallow that I could walk right onto the land.

I looked at the PadPad as I scrolled along the edge of the river. It led to a giant clearing in a valley. Descending towards the valley, I pushed the giant grasses aside and looked into the clearing. All sorts of creatures were in pens. It looked like a zoo. There was a conveyor belt that was dumping something into the pens of the creatures. I looked closely at the contents on the conveyor belt. It looked like bubbling green barf. It was really disgusting. The conveyor belt crawled to a stop. All of a sudden the Goldtromper rose out of a hole that was in the middle of the clearing. From my hiding place in the tall grasses, I could see him walk into a cave that was on the side of the clearing. I waited for two hours to make sure that the Goldtromper had gone to sleep in the cave. Finally I heard some snoring and after filing what I was hearing and seeing into my mask, I gingerly peered into the hole. I saw a ladder so I climbed down. When I reached the bottom of the hole, I looked around. It looked like a chemistry room. There were all sorts of containers. I picked up the bottle and read the label. It read, "Creatures will eat Padmin following consumption of this chemical." Another bottle read, "Creatures will grow to ten times their size following consumption of this chemical."

There was a creak and I looked at the stairs. I had awoken the Goldtromper! A golden foot was stepping down the ladder! I quickly glanced around the room and dove behind one of the chemical tables. The Goldtromper came down the ladder and started mixing chemicals together and putting them into a container. A pipe led from the container to the ceiling of the cavern. I heard a whirl. It sounded like the conveyor belt was starting back up. The Goldtromper must be mixing the chemicals and feeding them to the creatures that were penned up in the pens above me. The Goldtromper mixed the chemicals for a long time so I had a lot of time to look around. The cavern was about twenty foot long and twenty foot wide. It was twenty feet tall so the Goldtromper could easily fit into it. The fifteen foot tall shelves of chemicals were stacked along all the walls except one. The one bare wall had the ladder and the place where the chemicals were mixed. I became really dizzy from all of the weird chemicals' odors. I fell against one of the legs of the tables I was behind. All the chemicals clattered to the floor. The Goldtromper turned and moved towards me. He moved awkwardly because he was so large and I was able to slip past him and scramble up the ladder just as a thunderbolt shot out of the Goldtromper and hit where I had been moments before. I dashed into the woods at the end of the clearing and turned around to see what would happen next. I watched the Goldtromper slowly emerge from the hole. It lumbered to the edge of the clearing and looked around. Then it sulked around the pens and peered into them all. The Goldtromper looked like it didn't have good senses. I didn't stay to watch anymore. I ran down the path that I had come on to report my findings back to the village.

When I reached the shallow part of the river I walked across. I followed a path that was beside the bank for 2 hours, retracing my steps. Eventually, I came to the spot where I had seen the two Padmin conspiring against Womnolhi. Seeing their location reminded me of their conversation, and I hurried back to the village to let Womnolhi know of the conspiracy. I arrived at the village and Womnolhi came out to meet me.

"There were two Padmin that were talking about killing you tonight," I panted.

"Oh," replied Womnolhi calmly, "I'm sure you heard it wrong. Tomorrow is a festival for all Padmin. The winner of the festival is the person who scares me the most."

"But," I complained. "I'm worried."

"No complaining," Womnolhi retorted. "It will be fine."

I don't think that those two Padmin were just scaring Womnolhi. I think that they were conspiring with the Goldtromper to kill the only leader of the Padmin. Only tomorrow night would tell, but I needed to warn the other Padmin about it. I turned my helmet's microphone up so everyone could hear me. "Tomorrow Womnolhi will be killed! The village will be destroyed! Flee to the mines!" My voice boomed throughout the whole village.

All the Padmin started laughing. "He thinks that people will actually kill Womnolhi tomorrow."

"Ha, ha, it's just a joke."

"Ho, ho, that's hilarious."

"He thinks that tomorrow the king will actually die and that we will be attacked."

I sheepishly walked back to Womnolhi's house. "What will happen if you die tomorrow night, Womnolhi?" I asked with concern.

"An orange Padplant will be planted in the Padplant Palace by our god, Hoolip," replied Womnolhi. "When an orange Padmin is planted then that means that the current leader is dead. When an orange Padplant is planted, it is immediately ready to be picked. I have been alive for fifty two padyears which is a really long lifetime for a Padmin. If you live for a long time then you are favored by the gods. Most Padmin only live for about forty padyears." Womnolhi began droning on about the gods. I really didn't care, I was worried about him! I pretended to listen, just to be polite. "We have five gods. Hoolip is the god of Padplants. When an orange Padmin dies, Hoolip is the god who plants the orange seed. He is the god of the blue and yellow Padmin. Felag is the god of war. He is the god that helps us fight our enemies. He is the red Padmin's god. Hatein is the god of evil. He loves to send troubles against us. Wumblya is the goddess of love and beauty. She is the goddess of the trees. She is the goddess of the green Padmin. Gatno is the god of mining and engineering. He is the god of the grey and white Padmin. When a Padmin dies they become a star. If you are sinful then you become an evil creature."

"Wow," I exclaimed, Well, I think you are wrong about this threat being a joke. They seemed very serious!"

When I woke up the next morning, I felt restless and worried. After a hurried breakfast, I went over to Womnolhi's house, to stand guard and help in any way possible. Padmin were sneaking over to Womnolhi's house and were trying to scare him. Some of the Padmin had masks on. I saw that some pink Padmin were disguised as a huge flying creature. There were pretending to eat other pink Padmin. I was really sad that all these celebrating Padmin would die today, if I couldn't help prevent the attack. I went over to the shouting rock to try to warn the Padmin again. About one hundred Padmin were gathered there and they looked like they were waiting for someone.

"Why are you standing around the rock?" I asked.

"We are going to the mines," one of them answered. Apparently some Padmin had heeded to my warnings!

"We believe you!" they shouted.

"Flee to the mines!" I shouted. They all ran down the path that led to the mines. I gave a final plea to Womnolhi and the rest of the Padmin but to no avail. I felt a bit better than the night before, at least some of the Padmin believed me! As the Padmin ran towards the mines, I headed down the path to the shed to grab my cart. I loaded the Neutrizer into it. Running back to my house, I grabbed a supply of food and headed for the mines. I remembered that I needed the Cantseeum, so I ran back and added that to my already full cart. You may not remember this but the Cantseeum makes the planet invisible by sending out harmless blocking rays. If there was no hope I would smash the Cantseeum into pieces, so NASA would see the planet. I don't want to smash the Cantseeum if we survived, because I don't know what the humans will do to the Padmin. I didn't want the humans to kill the Padmin, just so they could build a colony here. Humans are pretty selfish, and had done similar things when discovering America and other continents. I would rather die than have humans kill all the Padmin and extinguish their race.

I arrived at the mines. I found that the other Padmin had told the workers in the mine to stay in the mine. They must have also told the tree chopping Padmin, because many green Padmin were there. I stepped onto the elevator with my cart and descended into the cavern. Hundreds of Padmin were gathered in the cavern. "Go warn the laboratory and the farms and tell them to come here," I commanded the nearest pink Padmin. He quickly flew up the elevator shaft. The Padmin were chattering. I cranked the volume on the microphone inside my helmet. "Everyone calm down." I pleaded. Everyone quieted down abruptly. "I am going back to the base to see if I can get anymore Padmin to come. It may be that I can convince a few. Please remain calm and in order while I am gone." I pushed my cart to the side of the cavern and stepped back onto the elevator platform and pulled the cord. I slowly rose. When the elevator stopped at the top of the elevator shaft I stepped off. I walked back to the village. I desperately needed the other Padmin to come, because the end was near. I broke into a run. I hope I am not too late. Suddenly, a cluster of forty white Padmin flew past me. Several blue, red, and yellow Padmin followed them. *At least some Padmin will be saved,* I thought. As I neared the village screams broke through the air. I slowed down and turned off the path to hide behind one of the houses on the outskirts of the village. There were giant creatures stomping all over the buildings! I looked towards the Shed. It had one side crashed in. Almost all the Padmins' houses were trampled. I saw a giant creature trampling Womnolhi to death.

Tears came to my eyes. There was nothing that I could do. All sorts of creatures were there. Many of the creatures I had never seen before. I was scared and beside myself with sadness. I quickly sprinted to the mines and told the Padmin what had happened. Everyone started moaning.

"They should have come here," wailed one of the Padmin.

"Hatein must be mad at us," said another.

"What have we done to deserve this?"

For hours we felt vibrations from the destruction of the village. Would these hideous creatures ever stop? Around nightfall it became quiet and I ventured up the shaft to view the damage. As far as the eye could see, everything had been flattened and destroyed. The creatures were gone. My bodyguards, who I had brought along, were extremely sad and some of them burst into tears again. I decided to go back to the cave and get some sleep. I arrived at the cave safely and in a few minutes the cave was filled with the sound of about 300 sleeping Padmin.

Chapter 7

I awoke the next morning to the sound of complaining Padmin. The Padmin were starving, so I decided to go to the village to get some food. "Are you scared?" I asked the red Padmin that were pulling the elevator up and down.

"No," one of them replied. "The creatures don't know that the mine is here. The insane human/Goldtromper thinks that this is an abandon mine. He won't bother us here. The only thing is that we don't have food here. We also don't have a way of growing Padplants. The god Hoolip can only plant Padplants in the ground that the Padplant Palace is built on."

"Oh," I replied. I felt a little better. The creatures couldn't find us, so the Padmin were mostly safe. I went back to the village. The village was deserted. Almost all the buildings were trampled. I went to the farms and gathered as many glowing glowma that could fit into the cart. I hurried back to the mines so I wouldn't meet any hostile creatures. When I delivered the cart of glowma to the hungry Padmin they all let out a cheer and rushed forward. I handed out the food and they were all thankful. It was late so all the Padmin settled down and went to sleep. I made one last run back to the village to get all of my "human" food from my house. To my dismay there was no sign of my food and my house had been leveled to the ground. I walked back to my cave feeling ready to go home.

"We should wait one more day to leave the cave," I told the restless Padmin as soon as I got back to the cave. Everyone listened to me. They recognized me as their leader now that Womnolhi was dead. I was really bored. "Where are my bodyguards?" I asked. All 120 of them stepped forward. I couldn't believe that they all were there. "We are going to the village," I explained. "We need to scout out the village to see if it is safe for the rest of us to come."

"Ok," they all replied in unison. I noticed that about one third of the Padmin in the cavern were my body guards. The Padmin and I got onto the elevator. When the elevator reached the top of the elevator shaft, the Padmin and I stepped off and started walking towards the village. When we got to the village all the Padmin started shouting in anger. I walked over to the Padplant Palace. It was in a wreck. I picked all the plants that were ready to be picked, even though there were only fifteen. Then I came to the last plant that looked like it was ready to be picked. I pulled and up popped an orange Padmin. I was overjoyed. I ran to tell my bodyguards. I didn't even have to, because they had seen their leader popping up. They all ran towards me with shouts of joy. The Padmin and I scooped up the orange Padmin and raced him back to the mines to show the other Padmin the happy news that a new leader was born. When we stepped of the elevator onto the floor of the cavern all the Padmin rushed forward.

"What is your name?" I asked the orange Padmin.

"Aforot," he replied.

I put the orange Padmin on my shoulder and shouted, "He said that his name was Aforot."

The Padmin all started talking at once. "Long live King Aforot."

"Hoolip has sent us a new leader!"

"Hooray!"

"Who will teach this new leader in all the ways of the Padmin?"

"I will choose someone," I shouted over all the noise of the shouting Padmin. All the Padmin stopped talking. "I will randomly choose one of you." I surveyed the room. I saw a pink Padmin sitting in one of the corners of the cavern. "I choose that one," I shouted as I pointed at the Padmin. He got up and walked towards me. "You will teach the orange Padmin the ways of your kind. You must teach him, for you are the only one that can do it.

"Ok," the Padmin answered calmly. "I am Gulpoy. I am fifty padyears old."

"He's fifty years old!" I shouted to the other Padmin. They gasped. I guess fifty is really old in padyears.

"I am the chief of the laboratory. When the pink Padmin have a question they ask me," Gulpoy replied. "I would be happy to train our next leader."

Some of the Padmin complained, but then they realized that this Padmin was actually the best option. After all, Gulpoy was one of the oldest of all the Padmin. Gulpoy led Aforot to one side of the cavern. "Five Padmin of every color must follow Aforot wherever he goes. Never lose sight of him," I told the Padmin. Five Padmin of every color immediately followed Aforot. It was getting dark outside so we went to sleep.

The next morning I took my body guards and walked to the elevator. "We are going to attack the insane creatures," I told the Padmin. "Follow me and I'll throw you when a creature comes."

We stepped off the elevator and walked down the path that led to the village. When we got to the village we meet a giant spider-like creature which was called a Spiwalker. I threw twenty red Padmin onto the body of the creature. I started throwing grey Padmin onto the legs. The creature crumpled to the ground. It would have taken too much time to bring it back to the Neutrizer so we just kept on walking down the path that led to the river. I should have used this path when I scouted on the Goldtromper, but I had not noticed it before. As we neared the path that led to the Goldtromper's base, we meet a herd of about fifty small Golumpets. These Golumpets were only one foot tall. I threw a Padmin onto each one. If I threw the Padmin just right then the Golumpet would splatter. Only two red Padmin died in the fight.

Suddenly, I looked up and saw a giant space ship come shooting into the atmosphere of the Padmins' planet. I ran towards the place where the UFO looked like it would land. Two green creatures stepped out. They looked around and walked towards me! They looked like a 5 foot tall walking octopus with arms. I quickly gathered my Padmin and we sprinted to hide behind some trees. The octopus creatures knew exactly where we were. They seemed to have x-ray vision. The Padmin and I hurried back to the village darting from tree to tree. The creatures gave up the hide and seek game and started walking towards the Goldtromper's base. "Stay here," I commanded to the nervous Padmin. "I am going to see what those green creatures are doing at the Goldtromper's base."

"Ok," Blue Leader replied.

I walked back towards the spot where the creatures had landed. I followed the path that the creatures took after they chased us. The path led towards the Goldtromper's base. I snuck up to the Goldtromper's clearing. I pushed the foliage aside and looked at the Goldtromper's base. The Goldtromper was standing and talking to the creatures. The hairless one-eyed creatures had two arms and eight legs. They looked like upright pale green octopi. They moved forward by walking with all eight legs. Thankfully they were talking loudly so I was able to hear what they were saying.

"So you got my message," the Goldtromper spoke. "I'm glad you could come so quickly."

"Yea," replied one of the Padmin. "As soon as you called we came. By the way my name is Hanpolot. This is Adopopie." Hanpolot pointed at the creature next to him.

"What do you want us to do?" asked Adopopie.

"I need you to help me kill all the Padmin," replied the Goldtromper. "I hate Padmin."

"Why?" asked Hanpolot.

"Don't ask questions!" snapped the Goldtromper.

The creatures turned around and looked right at me. I froze in terror. The two creatures started scampering towards me. I ran in fright towards the abandoned Padmin village glad to have two legs instead of eight like those green creatures. It made walking a lot faster. I whistled when I got back to the village and all my Padmin ran towards me. We ran down to the mines, boarded the elevator and went into the cavern. All the Padmin were nervously chattering. "What are you worried about?" I asked.

"We want to go home!" shouted one of the closer Padmin.

"Yeah!"

"Only the grey Padmin like it down here!"

"We don't want to stay here any longer."

"Ok," I hollered above the din. "But there are two new creatures that have just landed on your planet. They are one eyed green things."

"Those are the Hopgulies from our neighboring planet."

"We used to be able to call them with a device, but the Goldtromper took it because he thought it was human food," said one of the pink Padmin.

"Oh, so that's how the Goldtromper called those creatures," I spoke to no one in particular. All the Padmin took turns boarding the elevator and rising to the top of the cavern and disappearing to the top of the planet. All the white Padmin just flew through the opening. None of my bodyguards left me. "Go to the village," I told my Padmin. "I am going to talk to those green creatures. Stay at the village and defend it until I come back."

"Ok," they all replied in unison.

I rode the elevator to the top of the elevator shaft. I walked to the village and went to the Goldtromper's base to talk to the Goldtromper and to the Hopgulies. I found them standing in the Goldtromper's clearing; "I want to talk!" I hollered into the clearing. "I want the Padmin to be free. Can we work out a deal?"

"Ok," the Goldtromper replied. "You can come into the clearing."

"Ttyrhg kjaueyf jfygj fgtej jaopyut ggfter," the Goldtromper told the Hopgulies.

I think he was translating my words for the Hopgulies to understand, because after the Goldtromper stopped talking the Hopgulies started speaking. "Populy atha eiathas ihasoi awyoh ayhuv qmzhtygv." the Hopgulies exclaimed.

"Ok," the Goldtromper turned towards me, "If you show me how to get back to earth and leave the planet with the Hopgulies then I will order my creatures to stop attacking the Padmin. You will need to be a prisoner of the Hopgulies, though. If you do all this then I will leave the planet and leave the Padmin alone! Now is the moment of victory!" He triumphantly shouted.

"Ok," I replied. "I will talk to the Padmin about my decision."

I walked back to the village. "I am going to give you your freedom!" I shouted over the working Padmin who were trying to rebuild their houses after the destruction of their village.

A giant shout arose from the Padmin who had stopped working to cheer. "I will have to become prisoners of the Hopgulies to save your lives."

The Padmin stopped cheering. Sobs now reigned supreme. Gilroy and Aforot walked up to me and hugged my legs. "Thanks for all the help in saving our country," whimpered Gilroy.

"Thank you," Aforot cried. "I hope you get back to your planet somehow."

I cried, too. I had grown to love these little creatures. If I had talked to an insect on earth, I would be in the emergency room by now from fright. These creatures had not only taught me leadership skills, but they also helped me conquer my biggest fear. I went to sleep on the ground of the mine that had once been my house. The Padmin slept all around me. For the next two days, I rebuilt my space ship with the help of the Padmin. The Goldtromper came to check on my progress. He seemed satisfied and didn't eat any Padmin while he was their.

Two days after I talked to the Hopgulies I got ready to go. I got my PadPad and went towards the path that led the Goldtromper's hideout. "Goodbye," I cried as I walked down the path that led to the Goldtromper base. "I hope you rebuild your village soon."

All the Padmin started crying. All the Padmin, which is about four hundred gathered behind me and waved until I was out of sight. I walked to the Goldtromper's base. When I arrived I spoke, "The spacecraft is ready for use. All you have to do is turn the key and you will fly to earth. The food is in the spaceship. I want to see you tell the creatures not to attack the Padmin."

"Ok. Don't attack the Padmin, creatures," the Goldtromper said. "Now swallow this pill so you can understand the Hopgulies." He handed me a pill and I suspiciously took it and swallowed it. Instantly, I could understand the Hopgulies.

The Goldtromper screeched, "Now you will die on the Hopgulies planet. Mwah ha ha ha ha!"

Chapter 8

The Hopgulies looked at me, pulled out some sort of gun, and shot a laser beam at me. That was the last thing that I remembered from the planet of the Padmin. When I awoke from my sleep, I surprisingly felt ok. I appeared to be in a spacecraft of some sort. One of the Hopgulies was looking at me. "Hi, I'm Hanpolot," the creature said. "The other Hopgulies' name is Adopopie. We are bringing you to our planet, Hyasdig, on our spacecraft called Fastma. I think you humans call our planet Uranus. No human has ever seen us or our cities on Uranus. There is no uninhabited part on Uranus. We have built our buildings around the whole planet."

Wow, I thought, *No human has ever seen the surface of Uranus.* As I was thinking about what I had learned about Uranus in the University of Space Exploration, I looked around the room. Adopopie and Hanpolot were sitting in spinning chairs which were on opposite sides of the room. The spacecraft was round and had a half sphere on the top of the craft that was clear. It looked like the average alien spacecraft that you see in picture books as a kid. There were buttons all around the room and lights were blinking everywhere. The spacecraft had a diameter of about nine feet. From the floor to the top of the half sphere it was eight feet tall. I was lying in the middle of the room. It looked like the panel under me could open. I looked around the room as I slowly drifted off to sleep.

After about two hours I awoke from a blow to the spacecraft. "We have landed on Hyasdig. Be careful as you exit the premises," Hanpolot added.

What Hanpolot told me to do was extremely hard. The floor that I was lying on opened and I tumbled onto the ground. The two Hopgulies laughed and walked down a ramp that had lowered when the spacecraft had landed. I followed the Hopgulies down a steel pathway that led away from the landing area. On both sides of the walkway were walls that were three feet tall. I went to the wall on the left and looked over. About two feet down there was water that was boiling and bubbling. Steam was rising up from the top of the water. Thankfully, if I fell in my spacesuit could withstand the heat and the water. "Wow," I exclaimed. "Is that water really hot?"

"Yeah," Hanpolot replied. "If you fall in then you'll be boiled alive. Thousands of years before the giant flood swept across the surface of Uranus, we built our houses. The water covered the bottom floor of all the buildings. When the floods came we built walkways that have pillars that float on top of the water. The structure that we just left is where we park all of our Fastmas."

I turned and looked at the structure we had just left. It was a giant octagonal shape that had at least fifty Fastma which were parked randomly around the structure. I noticed that the two Hopgulies had gotten way ahead of me. I ran down the path and caught up to them. A giant city loomed in front of us. I heard a noise like a giant spring being released. "Those noises are the sounds of our guns. There is a civil war that is raging at our capital Hapmafobo," Adopopie spoke suddenly. "For many months the Gofdo group has been fighting the Fretito group.

The Fretito group stands for freedom. The Gofdo group is the stronger group of Hopgulies who want to suppress the weak among us. The Gofdo are not very smart. We are part of the Fretito group and most of the Fretitos are engineers. If you help us defeat the Gofdos then we will send you back to your planet. The Gofdos have a base on the other side of the city. In the meantime, we will treat you as a friend and not as a foe."

As we got closer to the city, I looked around. I had been to Venice as a child and Hapmafobo's waterways looked a lot like it. There were no boats but there were bridges everywhere. Most of the buildings were eighty feet tall. They looked like they were made out of steel. At one of the buildings a bunch of Hopgulies were scurrying out of it holding guns that looked like futuristic pistols. The building was all green, looked like a medieval castle. It was about one hundred feet tall and the front of the building was about two hundred feet wide. "The guns that the Hopgulies are carrying are called thor," Adopopie announced. "They shoot little balls called fars which paralyze whomever they hit. If a thor shoots you in the arm your arm would be paralyzed for the next seven days. If you are shot in the same spot before a week is over then that arm is paralyzed for life."

A giant ray of light sped past us and hit the wall behind us. "That was a fars. It almost hit your foot. Quick run into the Casmatle!" shouted Hanpolot. He and Adopopie ran into the building that looked like a castle. I sprinted. I was much faster than the two Hopgulies, so I easily got into the building before them. After all, two legs are better than eight. When Adopopie and Hanpolot entered Hanpolot panted, "This is the headquarters of the Fretito. Follow me as we enter."

I followed the two Hopgulies down a dark passageway. "I can make things appear when I think about them," Hanpolot instructed. "Watch this."

He clapped his hands and a boomerang shaped weapon appeared. "I just made a boomerang."

"Hey," I piped up. "That's what we call that type of a toy on earth, but we certainly can't make things appear!"

"Well stand back," he told me. He threw the boomerang down the hallway. It came back. A giant flamed leaped up along the ground in the hallway. The fire stretched down the hallway for about twenty feet. The boomerang came back to Hanpolot. "Don't worry," he comforted. "I hit a button on the side of the wall that makes the fire stop for five minutes, so that we can get across. The hallway has censors which picked up the movement of the things. The fire always burns unless someone hits the button on the other side of the fire. All of the traps in this walkway, help keep intruders out."

We walked down the passageway and we came to a pit of bubbling water. Hanpolot threw the boomerang at a button and a bridge appeared in front of us. We walked on through the tunnel. There was a moving platform which was going back and forth over a pit of lava. There was a floor that opened in front of us. At one part of the passageway giant steel beams fell in front of us. Each time there was a hidden button that Hanpolot hit in order to ensure a safe passage for us. I was so busy looking around that I forgot to ask where we were headed. Finally, after walking for about twenty minutes we came to a door. There was a message on the door which said: "Knock Twice." *I guess the pill that I swallowed let me read the Hopgulies' language, too,* I thought. *That might come in handy.* Hanpolot pushed another button which was hidden in the middle of the "o" in knock. Adopopie broke the silence. "If Hanpolot had knocked twice and hadn't hit the button then an electric ball would fall from the ceiling and electrocute us all to death." *Yikes, I* thought. *I'm glad that I didn't try to tackle this passage without my one-eyed octopus friends.*

The room that we entered was as tall as the Casmatle. At the top of the giant circular room there was a massive glass dome. I looked around. On one part of the room there was a long bar where a bunch of Hopgulies were sitting and eating some sort of meat. I looked at all the walls. Along the wall there was a ramp that spiraled to the top of the cylinder room. I craned my neck back and looked at the top of the one hundred foot ramp. I could see some Hopgulies going up and down the ramp. The middle of the Casmatle looked like a giant screw. In the center of the room there was a platform that was elevated ten feet off the ground. It had a ramp that led up to it. What a strange place!

As I was standing gazing at all the strange sights, the glass dome opened and a Fastma flew into the opening. It hovered onto a landing pad which was near the dome opening. Two Hopgulies fell out the bottom, as I had done hours before. Adopopie and Hanpolot who were watching me admire the place approached them. I followed. "Hello creature from another planet," they said to me." We are the leaders of the Fretitos. I am Golpet and this is Vomlon." Then he turned towards the rest of the Hopgulies and added, "Everyone listen to me!" Everyone turned their heads and that is when they noticed me. Every Hopgulie that was in sight of me turned and slithered towards me. Even the Hopgulies who were on the top of the ramp hurried down. Once everyone was gathered around me, Golpet spoke up above the hubbub from all the Hopgulies talking. "Listen to me my fellow rebels," he bellowed. "You all know that only a quarter of the city is on our side. Half of the city doesn't care who wins and the other quarter is the enemy." Golpet clapped his hands and a picture of a weird creature appeared on his hand. The creature looked just like the Hopgulies except it had two more arms and was musty yellow in color. All the Hopgulies growled so Golpet clapped and the image disappeared. It must be a Gofdo. Now Vomlon spoke, "As you all know, I am very old. Yesterday, I had a vision that a creature from another planet was going to come to our planet. He has come to free us from our oppressors. Let us all listen to him and take him as our new leader. He is from the land of the two legged creatures and comes with much wisdom from afar. We must listen to him now!" *I guess he must know about earth, I thought to myself. How? Did they spy on us? I would have to ask later. For now I needed to rise to the occasion and free these Hopgulies and get back to earth!*

"Hello Hopgulies," I hollered. "I am a human named Jackson and I will teach you some tactics that will help you defeat your oppressors." I was a very good public speaker. "If you show me the enemy base then I will destroy it."

All the Hopgulies cheered. They started talking amongst themselves.

"Did you hear that!" one of them explained.

"He will defeat the Gofdos for us!"

"Hurrah for Jackson!"

"Jackson will be our new leader!"

Vomlon loudly cleared his throat and the hubbub ceased. "I want Fory and Bilro to come forward please." Two of the Hopgulies stepped forward. "You will defend Jackson no matter what happens to him. Show him the enemy base and teach him in the ways of the Hopgulies."

"Yes, sir," replied the two Hopgulies and one of them spoke. "I am Fory and he is Bilro. Do you need anything?"

"Uh yeah, I'll need all sorts of things. Here I'll name them," I replied. I told him how to make a J-Bomb. I had invented this bomb when I was working in the University of Flying Spacecraft Laboratory by mixing some chemicals together. I tested my bomb in the Sahara desert. It blew an oasis clear off the face of the earth. The J-Bomb blows up a certain area of 300 square footage. Fory and Bilro hurried off towards the ramp. I walked over to Vomlon and asked, "Can I destroy all around the Godfos base, too?"

"Sure," Vomlon responded. "All around that area the Hopgulies are Godfos. The base is really hard to get into so be careful."

"Ok, thanks for the info."

I looked at the ramp the Casmatle and saw Fory and Bilro running down the ramp. When they reached me Fory said, "Follow me. All the materials that you requested have been brought to our laboratory."

I followed Fory and Bilro up the ramp. After walking up the spiraling ramp for about five minutes we came to a door which read, "Laboratory." I walked to the two foot wall that was on the edge of the ramp and looked over. I was about fifty feet in the air. I walked back to the door which had opened and followed Fory and Bilro into the room. As soon as I stepped into the room my heart leaped. The room was huge. It had more chemical filled beakers than I had ever seen in my life. There were pipes leading to almost everywhere in the room. I think I could spend the rest of my life in this room. The chemicals were all along the wall and in the center of the room there were tables that had test tubes and every type of scientific machine in the whole world. There were a lot of machines that I didn't know about. I looked at one of the tables and there were all the materials that I needed to make the J-Bomb. I got right to work. The two Hopgulies worked on something on one of the tables that had a bunch of machines that looked like computers. It was about noon and I finished by six o'clock. I was really hungry. "Hey, is there anything to eat?" I asked the two Hopgulies. Both of them jumped and turned.

"Yeah," Fory replied. "We can go eat at the cafeteria. Follow me." He walked out the door. I set the J-Bomb down on the desk and followed the two Hopgulies down the ramp and to the cafeteria on the ground level of the Casmatle. We sat down and Bilro touched a button on the table. In less than thirty seconds a waiter was at our table. "We will all have some tyfo please," Bilro told the waiter.

In one minute a very strange looking fish creature was set in front of us. The Hopgulies dug in with some forks that were sticking into the tyfo. I opened my helmet and took a small bite. It tasted just like beef for some reason. I was so hungry that I ate half of the tyfo. When our meal was done we stood up. "Do you want a tour of the city?" Bilro asked. "The Gofdos don't like to fight at night so the city is safe."

"Sure," I excitedly replied.

"Ok, follow me."

We walked down the passageway. It was much easier because the buttons were much more accessible. We left the building and walked onto the sidewalk. We walked until we got to a building that was surrounded by water with only a small passageway that led to a door. The building was about fifty feet tall and was all pale green except it was black around the door. I saw a lot of Hopgulies walking in and out of the building. "This is the Gofdo's base," Fory instructed. "You can blow it up tomorrow."

"Ok," I replied. "If I blow it up will you let me fly home?"

"Yeah, Vomlon agreed to that," answered Bilro.

"Ok, well I'll need a flying space craft that can drop things. Do you have one?" I asked.

"Uhh, yeah," said Bilro. "The Fastma can drop things from low altitudes. We can be ready to fly over the base in two days. It takes our mechanics a long time to prepare the Fastmas for flight. Let's go back to the Casmatle and sleep." We walked back to the other side of the city and entered the Casmatle. We walked down the passageway and entered the big room. I followed Fory and Bilro up the ramp until we were about one fourth of the way to the top. Bilro opened a door and we stepped into an extremely long room. It was so long that I could hardly see the other side, but it was only ten feet wide and ten feet tall. There were six foot long beds with no covers on the right side of the wall. I literally sank into a bed, because the mattresses were like jelly so that the sleeper's body could fit perfectly. Surprisingly the beds were comfortable and despite my suit I quickly went to sleep.

Chapter 9

The next morning I woke up to the movement of about three hundred Fretitos getting out of the beds and hurrying past my bed. All the Fretitos in that long room were hurrying past me and were walking out the door. I stepped into line and I finally made it down the ramp and to the cafeteria where almost every Fretito was sitting. I hit a button that was in front of me. A waiter hurried over. I ordered a tyfo, because it was the only food that I knew the name of. After I was done eating I looked around and saw Bilro and Fory beckoning me from the entrance of the ramp. I followed them and they led me to a door. I opened it and an amazing sight greeted my eyes. The fifty square foot room had shelves all along 3 sides of the room. On the shelves there were all sorts of guns. I picked up one. "Can you show me how to shoot this?"

"Sure," Bilro replied. "That guns a gump. Come with me." I followed Bilro to the wall that had ten doors instead of weapon shelves. Bilro opened the first door and we stepped inside. It was a hallway that was fifteen feet long. It had a target at the end. I lifted the gump and pulled the trigger. A giant beam of light shot down the hallway and hit the target. The target was made out of a gel like material so when I shot the bullet just went right through the target and got stuck in the gel. I could still tell where the bullet hit, though. In about ten seconds the bullet hole filled in with more gel. "Don't worry about shooting too much at the target," Bilro informed me. "The gel substance is about ten foot long, so the bullet is mostly stopped before it reaches the outer wall."

"Ok," I cheerfully replied. For the next ten hours I tried out all the guns. I wasn't even bored. I had always liked guns. Finally, after trying out many guns I picked a gun which looked like a pistol except inside the barrel there was a green watery material. The label on the gun said it was a huli. When I shot it the bullet went so fast that I couldn't even see it. I shot it twenty five times and then it stopped shooting. "Why did my gun stop?" I asked Fory who was also practicing with a bazooka type gun.

"It means that you're out of bullets," Fory answered. "The bullets are over there." He pointed to a table that had a bunch ammunition clips on it. I went to the container that read, "HULI BULLETS." I pulled seven cartridges out of the jar and put them into my pockets. Then I pushed the eject button on my gun and a cartridge fell out the bottom of it. I saw a conveyor belt that had a sign above it. The sign read, "Put the empty cartridges here." I put the empty cartridge on the conveyor belt and the conveyor belt started moving. I watched as the cartridge went through the wall and I heard it fall with a metallic crash. I strapped a super strong piece of Velcro that was on my vest over my huli to keep it in place. "I'm going to go get something to eat and then I really want to see the city again," I told Bilro and Fory who were still trying out guns.

"Ok, we'll go, too," they both replied in unison. We walked out the door and down the ramp. We walked to the bar and sat on three of the four hundred seats. Fory hit a button and the waiter came. "I would like a grop," Bilro instructed.

"So would I," Fory spoke up.

I didn't know what to order. I suddenly remembered the old saying, "when in Rome do as the Romans do," and ordered a grop as well.

When the grop came it was 1 foot long. It had a huge eye in the front of its body. The eye took up the whole face of the fish like creature. It had gills which had two forks sticking out of them. It had only one fin which was on its tail. The tail looked like a whale's tale. I picked up one of the forks that protruded from the midsection of the grop. I took a bite. It tasted like bacon, which is one of my favorite foods. I quickly ate the whole grop in less than five minutes. The Hopgulies at the bar stared at me as I gobbled down my food and asked for another one. After my third grop I was feeling really sick. I needed a walk so I asked, "Hey Bilro and Fory. Can you guys show me around the city? After eating all that grop I need to do some walking."

"Sure," Fory replied. "I can, but Bilro needs to get everyone ready for tomorrow." Fory led me to the passageway that led out of the Casmatle. When we arrived at the door that led to the street Fory exclaimed, "Do you want to see where all the Hopgulies are made?"

"Yeah. You guys are made?" I inquired. I didn't really believe him.

"Yes," he replied. "We all come out of a little hole in the ground. Follow me." We walked to the middle of the city where there was an eighteen foot tall volcano in the middle of the walkway. "This is where we are born," Fory said. "It used to be much taller but the flood made us build this platform so now the Spawner, that's what we call it, seems much smaller. Since the Spawner is partly under water it has been spawning evil Gofdos. When the water is cleared away from the volcanoes then no more Gofdos will come out."

"I can easily make the water disappear with the right materials," I instructed Fory. "I will need sheets of steel and a pump."

"Ok," Fory replied. "I can get those materials for you by tomorrow. I will need to get them from the Fopoto."

"What is the Fopoto?"

"That's the manufacturing plant of the Fretitos. That is where every material that the Hopgulies know about is stored. We get our steel from the planet Fhjaayton, I think you humans call it Pluto."

"Wow," I replied. Suddenly a Gofdo climbed out of the Spawner and rushed towards us. Thankfully I had clipped the huli onto my suit, because now I desperately needed it. I unstrapped the Velcro strap which was around my huli and lifted the gun and pulled the trigger. The invisible bullet must have hit the Gofdo, because it screamed and sank to the ground. As soon as the Gofdo screamed at least twenty Gofdos hurried towards us. Fory and I ran for the Casmatle. One of the Gofdos threw a glowing staff at Fory and it hit him in the leg. He fell to the ground and I quickly bent down to help him. He couldn't walk so I threw him over my shoulder, and hurried towards the Casmatle. The Gofdos were right behind me. I entered the door of the Casmatle and hurried down the passage way. I shot the button and ran across the fire trap. I thankfully managed to hit all the buttons with my gun, so I didn't die in any of the traps. I finally entered the big room and set Fory down on one of the seats that was pushed up to the bar. I hit the button and a waiter came. "I would like some water please," I instructed the waiter. Water was brought to me. I was extremely thirsty. The water was served in a bowl. I gave one to

Fory who gratefully took it. I drank my bowl and each time I asked for more. I drank at least twelve bowls of water, which is probably equivalent to a half a gallon. I was really tired, but I needed to get Fory to a medical place so he could get healed. "Where do you get healed from injuries Fory," I asked.

"Uhh," he answered. "Walk up the ramp and I will tell you which room it is in. I lifted Fory onto my shoulders and walked up the ramp. Fory was surprisingly light for something that was about 5 foot tall. "Here is the door," Fory spoke up. I opened the door which read, "1". When I opened the door there was a row of chairs. "Set me down here, Jackson," Fory commanded. "This is where you wait to get treated. Go tell Vomlon about your plan to get the water away from the Spawner. He is in room 169 which will be about three fourths of the way up the ramp."

"Ok," I said. "See you tomorrow." I walked up the ramp. 56, 57, 58. I walked on, 78, 79, 80. I had walked for about seven minutes when I finally reached the door which read, "169". I opened the door and stepped in. The room was dimly lit. As my eyes adjusted to the darkness I saw two thrones at the back of the room which Vomlon and Golpet were sitting. I walked to the thrones which were about fifteen feet away and announced, "I can make the water go away from the Spawner if I can just have a lot of steel and a pump."

"Really!" exclaimed Golpet incredulously. "I will send a message to the Fopoto to get you a pump and as much steel as you want. I'll have them deliver it to the Spawner. I will send one hundred Fretito fighters to defend you. You only have fifteen minutes before the Gofdos will be too powerful for us. The steel should be there in five minutes. Hurry to the Spawner so you can get the water away tonight. The one hundred Fretito soldiers will guard you."

"Thank you so much," I replied. I had to hurry because it was almost dark. I quickly walked down the ramp. I walked down the passageway that led out of the Casmatle and went into the center of the city where the Spawner was. When I got to the Spawner, the steel and the one hundred Hopgulies were already there. Thankfully my suit was waterproof. I took a sheet of steel and climbed down a ladder that led into the boiling water. I planted the sheet into the ground. The sheet was five feet tall. Thankfully the water was only four foot high. In the next ten minutes I put all the sheets of steel around the Spawner. The pump had two hoses. I took the pump underwater and put one hose by the Spawner. I took the other hose and put it on the other side the steel wall. I climbed the ladder for the last time. Suddenly two hundred Gofdos appeared from the direction of their base. I took out my huli and blasted away. I killed at least 10 Gofdos. 12 Fretitos lay dead so I shouted, "To the Casmatle!"

All the Fretitos turned and fled. I reached the door about a minute before the Fretitos got there. We all rushed down the passage way. One of the Fretitos fell onto the stake trap and was impaled, because he didn't run fast enough. He was dead so we walked on with a heavy heart. We had lost about fourteen Fretitos because one Fretito had been killed on the way to the Casmatle. We entered the big room and I went straight to the bed area and went to sleep.

The next day I awoke, got out of my bed, and walked to the bar. I hit the button and a waiter came over. "I would like a tyfo please," I told the waiter just as Fory and Bilro walked up.

They sat down on some of the stools and Fory spoke, "Hey Jackson. Today we are going to bomb the Gofdos base." Fory pointed at the platform that was in the middle of the huge room. "Can you go stand on that platform and tell all the Fretitos that are present the plan for today?"

"Sure," I replied. I got up and walked up the steps that led to the top of the platform. I leaned on the railings and shouted, "Can everyone hear me?" All the Hopgulies in the room turned and looked at me. Then they all came and crowded around the platform that I was standing on. I looked over the mass of Fretitos and spoke again. "Today I am going to free you from the tyranny of the Gofdos."

"Good job, Jackson!"

"He will free us!"

"Go Jackson!"

I paused until the cheering died down. "I will need help, though." I think that the Hopgulies are one of the most interruptive people in the universe.

"We will help you!"

"Yeah!"

"Everyone help Jackson!"

I paused once again while the Hopgulies shouted. "Can everyone please be quiet?!" I hollered.

"Sure!"

"Of course we can be quiet!"

"You should have told us?!"

"We'll be quiet!"

After about one minute the Hopgulies stopped talking about how they would be quiet. I decided just to talk right through them. "When I blast a hole in the Gofdos base then you need to rush into the base and kill everyone in it. Get ready to go. Meet me here when you are done."

As the Fretitos trickled slowly away I went to the gun room and got seven more packs of ammunition for my huli. I met about eighty other Hopgulies who were also picking out their guns. I went back down the spiraling ramp and went up to Fory and Bilro who were talking amongst themselves. "Did you guys load the J-Bomb onto your Fastma?"

"Yup," Bilro replied. "Here is a yellfone. When you talk into it we will bomb the door of the Gofdos base. Then you can rush in." The Hopgulies all started trickling back around the platform. When almost all of the four hundred Fretitos were there Golpet, who had just exited the spiraling ramp, went up to the platform and shouted, "Jackson will be your leader while you are attacking the Gofdos base. If you disobey him it is like disobeying me. Do you understand?"

The Hopgulies all gave their two cents. "Of course we will listen!"

"Who do you think we are?!"

"We'll listen!"

"We can destroy the Gofdos!"

"Three cheers for Jackson!"

"Hip, hip, hooray!"

I sighed and walked to the passageway. The Hopgulies all followed me. We made it safely through all the traps and out of the Casmatle. The Hopgulies started walking to the Gofdos base. "Come back guys," I said. "We need to spread out so that the Gofdos won't get suspicious. I'll meet you at the Gofdos' base in five minutes. Fory and Bilro you go to the Fastma and get ready to bomb the entrance. The rest of you spread out and start heading towards the Gofdos base."

All the Hopgulies, except for Bilro and Fory who walked towards the Fastma landing spot, started walking towards the Gofdos' base. I started running towards it. When I arrived 200 Fretitos were already there. I talked into my yellfone, "Drop the bomb!"

Just then a Fastma flew over the heads of the surprised Fretitos and dropped my J-Bomb onto the entrance of the Gofdos' base. A giant explosion occurred. As soon as the smoke cleared, even I was surprised. Twenty feet of the Gofdos' base had been evaporated by the J-bomb. It was really strange, because you could see into the rooms which were fifty feet in the air. It looked like a knife had cut the front of the building off. I charged into the base and the Fretitos fighters followed close behind. For such talkative creatures the Hopgulies fought really well. We were able to force ourselves into a large room that was much like the huge room that was Casmatle. There were all sorts Gofdos who were shooting at us with these guns that were like extremely fast shooting bazookas. Fretitos were falling dead all around me so I decided that I had to destroy the Gofdos' base alone.

Chapter 10

I told everyone to get out of the building. Everyone hurried out and ran to hide behind some building that were about twenty yards away from the Gofdos base. Fory and Bilro had parked their Fastma by a landing pad that was next to the enemy base. They were still in it so I ran up to the glass and pounded on it. "Let me in guys." They opened the bottom of the Fastma, so I walked in and went over to Fory and Bilro who were looking at the Gofdos base. "Can you tell me how to fly the Fastma? I need it really badly." I panted. All this fighting was making me tired. I desperately wanted to go home to my family.

"Sure," replied Fory. "There is the gas pedal and there is the brake. Also….."

"That's all I need, thanks," I interrupted. "Hurry up and get off."

Bilro and Fory ran down the ramp that led out of the Fastma. I watched them as they went towards the group of Fretitos who were nervously gathered in a group. My plan was to fly the Fastma into the Godfos' base and then jump out. I looked at a screen that was next to me. It read, "Gas tank full." That was really good news. When I crashed the Fastma into the Godfos' base then the gas would start burning the building. I pressed the gas pedal and the Fastma shot upward. My hand slipped and accidentally hit a stick which shot the Fastma forward! I was about ready to crash into the base! I didn't know where the eject button was. *I should have listened to Fory and Bilro's explanation,* I thought. I hit the building going at about 100 miles per hour. The windshield cracked and glass flew all over me. The last thing that I remembered was a giant explosion which seemed to come from the right of me.

When I came to I couldn't see. There was something wet on my eyes. I heard beeping noises all around me. I tried to get up but something was holding me down. Suddenly I heard a shout. "He's alive!" It sounded like Adopopie. I heard a scuffling of hundreds of octopus feet moving towards my bed. "Take off the eye patch," commanded Vomlon. "Sit him up in his bed. I will explain what happened to him."

My bed started rising and one of the Hopgulies took off the thing that was covering my eyes. Slowly, the room came into focus. I saw that Vomlon, Adopopie, Golpet, Hanpolot, and twenty more Hopgulies which were crammed in the little area. I glanced around the room behind them. There was not a lot of light in the room, but I saw that there were different colored lights along the walls. Vomlon began to explain, "After the explosion you were thrown into the platform which led up to the Gofdos base."

I realized that the more important Hopgulies knew not to interrupt, but the other Hopgulies sure didn't. The other Hopgulies all started talking at once. "Yeah, I saw Jackson go flying."

"I know."

"It was crazy!"

"I think he was flying with his long arms."

"I wish I could fly."

"Yeah, me too."

"Maybe Jackson can teach us!"

"Yeah. Hurray for teacher Jackson."

"Everyone calm down," Golpet commanded. "No one can talk unless spoken to." All the Hopgulies slowly stopped talking. Golpet continued where Vomlon had left off, "So, after you landed on the platform, a giant piece of the base started falling towards you. Adopopie hurled himself towards you. He grabbed your suit and dragged you to safety just as the piece of wall crushed the spot where you were."

"Thank you Adopopie," I whispered. It really hurt to talk. Golpet went on speaking, "Adopopie brought you here to be worked on. The gas that you inhaled made you almost go blind. We were able to save you. We operated on your eyes. You have been recovering for two days already. Well, while you were being brought back to the Casmatle, the Fretito fighters were watching the fire destroy the Gofdos' base. Apparently, many of the Gofdos had inhaled the burning fuel and had died because of it. After the fire burned out, the Fretito fighters killed the rest of the Gofdos. We went through the city and killed every Gofdo. All the other Hopgulies are on our side now. Tomorrow you will be all ready to go home. We made a special spaceship that is programmed to bring you back to earth. Now we will leave so you can sleep. I'll turn the lights on."

My bed started to unfold. As the Hopgulies left, I looked at the screens all around the room that had all sorts of graphs and charts. Around the screens lights flashed. *All these screens must be monitoring me,* I thought. It felt good to be so well taken care of. I felt drowsy so I lay down and went to sleep.

The next morning, I awoke to the smell of fish in front of me. I slowly propped myself up and saw that a tray with food had been set next to me. As soon as I sat up the bed started to fold. The food tray was on a mechanical arm and it moved until it was directly under my head. There was a straw so I started sipping in the soup. It tasted like fish. It was really good even though I didn't really like fish. When I was done I pushed the tray away and untangled my feet from the sheets that enveloped me. I got out of bed and walked to the door which opened. I walked up the ramp to room 169 to see Vomlon and Golpet. When I opened the door they both jumped. "Hey guys," I said. "I am ready to go. Thanks for all that you did. Without you I would never have been able to get off the Padmins' planet."

"No, thank you," Golpet replied. "Without you we would have been killed by now. Now our city will live in peace. You are the hero of every true Hopgulie. Deep in our hearts you are our hero."

"I agree," agreed Vomlon. "If you aren't ever a hero on your planet just remember that you are still our hero. We will all remember you. Because of you all the Hopglies will live in peace. You just saved our planet! And for that we thank you. Now I will call all your friends so you can say goodbye. If I called everyone you would never leave because there would be so many goodbyes. We still love our fellow Hopgulies even though they talk a lot." Vomlon pushed a button that was on the arm of his chair and spoke, "I would like Adopopie, Hanpolot, Fory, and Bilro to come up see me."

In about five minutes the four Hopgulies were in the throne room. "I really like all of you guys," I cried. Tears were streaming down my face, knowing I would never see them again. "Thanks for everything that you did for me. I will always remember how you saved me from the Goldtromper.

Adopopie, I will never forget how you risked your life to save me from the falling wall."

The Hopgulies all started wagging their heads. "We will miss you too," they whimpered in unison. After five minutes of crying, it was time to go. The Hopgulies and walked to the Fastma landing sight. There was an eight foot tall capsule that looked like a lemon. It made out of yellow glass. I stepped up towards the contraption and a small panel opened. I climbed in. "Wait," Golpet shouted. "Before you go, we sent an invisible scout plane with Hopgulies who had invisible suits on to earth to make sure all was safe for your return. We just heard back that the Goldtromper has landed and is terrorizing the populous. Whoever he bites becomes a Goldtromper. We put a chemical in the drink of the President of the United States of America. The chemical made him have a dream about you coming. The actual dream was that someone named Jackson would come and save the world. He is ready to listen to you. The chemical made him listen to everything that you say."

So my adventure is not over yet? I thought to myself. *What's next?* Out loud I said, "Wow, that's awful. Goodbye friends. I hope that your planet lives in peace forever."

"Thanks to you, it will!" Vomlon spoke as the panel closed. I waved as the spacecraft blasted into the air. The spacecraft zoomed through the atmosphere. After traveling for two minutes I started getting bored so I thought about many things. I had been gone from earth for a month. I started thinking about my siblings, as I daydreamed about our happy reunion that would surely come soon. I had learned so much and now it was time to take on the Goldtromper one last time. Would my parents be ok after missing their son for so long?

What about my siblings? Hopefully they hadn't given up hoping for my return! Jenna at twenty-two is still living at home, but going to college at Michigan State University. Brandon an eighteen year old was just finishing with high school. Janessa is fourteen, Jordon is eight, and Weston is three. I especially miss Weston who is probably going to seem bigger and be talking more. Both of my parents are fifty. At twenty four, I am the oldest. I am sort of young for being a graduate at the University of Space Travel. Suddenly a voice spoke, "You are in Earth's atmosphere."

Really, I thought. *That was quick. This spaceship must go extremely fast.* The spacecraft stopped and the panel opened. Cameras flashed as I stepped off of the spaceship. A news reporter held a microphone up to my face and asked, "Are you Jackson?"

"Uhh," I stammered. "Yes I am. I hear that there is a creature that is terrorizing earth. Can I speak to President Henry?"

The crowd parted and President Henry Fremond walked through the crowd to stand in front of me. "Do you know how to kill this creature?" he asked.

"I think I have an idea." I replied.

The president straightened his tie. "The congress and I have decided to make an executive order. The USA will do whatever you say for one month. Wait, is your last name Williams?"

"Yes," I answered.

"So, you're the spaceman who went missing when you were trying to get to the moon. I so glad that you made it home. We sent two searching spacecraft that looked for you, but we couldn't find you."

"Yea, I was on an invisible planet or two." I replied casually.

There was a look of disbelief on the face of the president. "How can a planet be invisible? Oh, well. We need to focus on the problem at hand. Can you write a book about your adventures some day?"

"Sure," I replied. "Where will I sleep tonight?"

"You can go home. I will put you in one of my private helicopters and fly you home. You live in Kalamazoo, Michigan, right?"

"Yup," I replied. "Thanks so much."

A random person beckoned me to follow him, so I did through the crowd of reporters and people trying to get a look at me. I think the man I was following was a secret service agent because he had sunglasses on. I always wondered why secret service guys wear glasses. I researched it once when I had library time at school. It is for identification or something like that. The Secret Service guy and I walked for about five minutes until we arrived at a field that had a helicopter in the middle of it. We walked to the helicopter and stepped onto a platform to climb in. As soon as I stepped in the helicopter, it lifted from off the ground. I jumped as the secret service guy spoke, "Sorry that I couldn't talk. My name is Sandy Gordons, it's nice to meet you." He stretched his hand out.

I took it and exclaimed, "Nice to meet you as well."

"You must be Jackson Williams," continued Sandy. "You are all over the news around the world. When the creature came to earth he said that he escaped the planet, because of you. Everybody has heard about you. Almost all the countries of the world are ready to have your aid."

He paused so I said, "Can you tell me about the creature? The creature is called a Goldtromper. I know what he looks like because he was on the planet that I crashed onto, but what is he exactly doing?"

"Uh," Sandy began. "The creature has been going around biting people. These people turn into the creature when they are bitten. There are about fifty thousand of those Goldtrompers and they are growing in number by the day. Their camp is in Honolulu, Hawaii. They ate all the boats in Pearl Harbor and they devoured every living creature in the whole area. One survivor said that when they ate fish they could start swimming and when the Goldtrompers ate birds they started to fly."

"Wow," I interrupted. "They will be really hard to kill."

"Yea, I know. Well, the Goldtrompers are terrorizing the populous of all the Pacific Islands now. Tomorrow I will pick you up and we are going to go to the White House where you will meet with the United Nations. They are voting tonight to see if they will all listen to you. I am appointed to guard you. The pilot and I will sleep in the helicopter tonight. I will knock on your door at 8:00 tomorrow morning. I hope you have a good night."

The helicopter had landed. I stepped off of the helicopter which had landed in field which is in my parents' backyard. I kept my suit and the PadPad in the helicopter. I didn't have a house of my own, because I had slept on campus when I was schooling at the University of Space Exploration. The field was about 200 yards long and about 100 yards wide. My Dad said that it used to be a big potato field. I ran the short distance and arrived at the front door of the house. One of my five siblings must have seen me, because the door was thrown open and all of my three brothers and two sisters rushed towards me. My mom and dad came to the front door. None of us could speak because we were crying tears of joy. My family doesn't like to dwell on the sad things of life, so we stopped crying after about five minutes. My sibling started piling questions onto me.

"Where did you go?" inquired Janessa.

"Yeah, Makayla is really missing you," teased Jenna. Makayla was my fiancé.

"Really? She misses me?" I joked. "What a surprise! I missed her too!"

"God promised us that you would come back, Jackson. We didn't lose hope. I made a birthday cake, hoping that the day we would see you would be today, on your birthday," Mom gently spoke.

That's right! It was my Birthday! I had totally forgotten in my excitement to get home. "Hey,   son," Dad's   voice boomed. "So glad you could make it home." He walked up and put his hand on my shoulder. "We knew you would, too," he quietly told me.

"Come inside Jackson," Jordon pleaded.

"I wike the Xsphere. Wets go pway Jordon," whined Weston.

I groaned and followed my two youngest brothers into the house. "That cake looks too good to just leave it there, guys. Can't we eat the cake first," I pleaded as I looked at the carrot cake."

"Ok, whatever," Jordon rolled his eyes.

"Wow, miracles do happen I guess," laughed Brandon. "Those boys would never give up there Xsphere time."

My family gathered around the table. I noticed my sisters were missing. Where had they gone? I pulled back the chair that was in front of the cake, and tiredly sat down. It had been a long day. Suddenly the door burst open and Makayla, Jenna, and Janessa walked in. Jenna and Makayla are really close friends. They are both the same age. My heart skipped a beat. I pushed back my chair and ran to hug Makayla. "I didn't know that you were back to earth," Mackayla exclaimed as she giggled.

"Yup," I laughed. "I told the aliens that I needed to get home on my birthday. I told them that I had the most important thing in the world waiting for me when I got home."

I put my arm around Makayla and led her to the table where I sat down in front of the cake with Makayla next to me. We all happily sang happy birthday as the candles on the cake burned brightly. I read the icing which was printed neatly on the cake. It read, "Welcome back to earth, Jackson!"

"Are you one, are you two, are you three, are you four," everyone chanted. Finally we reached twenty five. Wow, I was getting old. I blew out the candles.

"What's your birfday wish, Jackson?" asked Weston.

"He isn't supposed to say it," scolded Janessa as she frowned.

"It's ok, Janessa. My wish is to never leave this planet again," I smiled as I looked at Makayla. For some reason my parents both looked at each other and smiled, too. They always smile when relationships are involved. My mom got a knife from the kitchen and cut up the cake. She put the carrot cake on plates which she passed to everyone who was seated around the table. I dug into my piece of carrot cake with fervor. Nothing tasted as good as carrot cake on the Hopgulies planet. I looked around the room. It was so good to be home. There was an island in the middle of the kitchen. Our dining room was connected to our kitchen. Our counters were all black marble. Our cupboards were mahogany. Our stove was across from our dishwasher. The sink was to the left of the dishwasher. The stove was a counter top stove, which was on the island. On the other side across from the island was the fridge which was against the wall. The oven was across the island to the right of the stove. Everything looked so normal. It gave me a sense of calmness that I hadn't felt in weeks.

"After tonight, I have to go to the White House," I told my family. "I need to sleep there so the creatures don't find me here and kill you and me."

"Why do you have to go to the White House tomorrow, Jackson?" asked Makayla. "You just got home!"

"Well, If I don't go then the creatures will come looking for me and I don't want to put any of you in danger," I replied. "I need to be at the White House for a month. I really want to stay home with you, but duty calls. I will have my cellphone on me, though. So we can talk every day, unless the Goldtromper eats me."

"What's a Goldtromper?" asked Jordon.

"That's the name of the creatures that are causing problems in Hawaii," I replied. Apparently my dad had not filled my younger brothers in on the news of the Goldtromper. He was probably worried about scarring them.

My dad looked worried. "But I heard that a Goldtromper ate Vecovis Sabitito. Will the Goldtromper version of Vecovis Sabitito be as smart as the human version, because the human version is one of the smartest people in the world?"

"Yeah, but the Goldtromper version will be even smarter," I explained. "I am going to have to put a block on my phone so he can't track my calls. I will also have to use all my brain power to come up with a tool that can destroy him."

Chapter 11

We had all finished our cake, so I said, "Hey, guys lets go play Xsphere." I might as well relax with these boys a bit. It would become time before I saw them again.

All the boys cheered. Even Brandon did, but he was mocking the other boys. As I walked down the stairs that led the Xsphere, I looked at all the pictures that were on the wall. My mom had put all our pictures up. They looked like steps going down. I was at the top, then Jenna, then Brandon, and so on. I had reached the bottom of the stairs so I walked down the hallway that led to a big room. I looked around the room. There was a door to my left, which was the bathroom. There was a door on the far end of the room which was the door that led to my bedroom. I walked around a corner and almost bumped into Brandon. "Here, take this," Brandon instructed as he handed me a mask. I put it on and I was in the steppes of Mongolia riding with Genghis Khan. After riding for about five minutes, I said, "This is really boring." All the riders turned to look at me.

"How dare you speak of the army in that way," shouted an angry man.

"Bring him to Genghis Khan," ordered one of the men.

I ripped off my mask just before the rough hands grabbed me. All my brothers had their masks off and were laughing at me. "The game wanted you to be bored," laughed Brandon.

"Wow, thanks guys. Can we do a peaceful game now?" I asked.

After much arguing amongst the younger two boys, they finally decided on this game that you had to build a city and that you were the mayor. I put my mask back on and I was suddenly in a room. I looked around the room and saw that I was sitting in a desk and that there was a map in front of me. "Where would you like that new park to be constructed Mayor Williams?" asked a woman who was standing in front of me.

"Uhh right here," I replied as I pointed at the map. "I think that that would be a good spot, because it is right next to a group of houses. I would also like a side walk that connects all the houses be also connected to the park."

I drank from a cup of coffee that was on the desk. "This is a really fun game," I whispered.

A man walked in and shouted, "So you're a fake, too. Well, I'll show you. Come with me. You're under arrest for pretending to be the mayor."

I ripped off my mask. "Why do I always mess up?" I asked my brothers who had taken their masks off as soon as they heard me take off mine. "You have to get used to it," Jordon instructed.

I stretched. "When I was your age we had these things called the Wii where you could play all sorts of really fun games. I think I like the Wii games more than the Xsphere games."

I walked back upstairs to go talk to the women. I sat down next to Makayla on one of the two couches that were in our family room. The family room had two couches and two chairs. My dad was sitting in his black easy chair. My mom was sitting in the love seat. Jenna was sitting on the other side of

Makayla and Janessa was lying on the couch. "Have you gotten your job yet, Jenna?" I asked. Jenna was trying to get a job at Goldels, which is a huge clothing store.

"Yea, thankfully Makayla helped me get the job," replied Jenna. Makayla is a manager at Goldels, even though she is only 23.

"Can you write a book about your travels?" my mom requested.

"Yeah, maybe after I destroy all the Goldtrompers," I replied.

It was about ten o'clock so Makayla got up and walked to the door. "Bye everyone, hope you have good luck, Jackson."

I ran over to her and gave her a hug. "I hope when I come back that we can get married," I told her.

Makayla's eyes started to tear up. "I hope you come back, Jackson."

"Don't worry, I will," I comforted.

I said goodnight to everyone and walked down to my room. I got into my pajamas. I pulled back the covers and stepped into bed. As I fell asleep I looked around the room. My bed was a queen bed which was really nice because I had a lot of space. I had a desk where my laptop was siting. Across from my bed there was a closet. To the right of my door there was a dresser. My eyelids felt heavy. I went to sleep.

The next morning I woke up and threw back the covers. I couldn't believe that I was on the Hopgulies planet just yesterday. I walked back upstairs and got some Cinnamon Toast Crunch from the cereal cupboard. I got a bowl and spoon and sat down. I was really surprised that Cinnamon Toast Crunch was still around because that was my favorite cereal when I was a kid. It still is now. *The Padmin love Cinnamon toast crunch too,* I thought. *That was funny to see the Padmin so excited.* By the time I had finished eating, all my family was in the kitchen eating their cereal. I finished my cereal and put my bowl into the sink. "Goodbye, everyone. Hope to see you in a month," I told them after a lot of hugs and well wishes. I turned to leave.

As I walked out the door, I tried to swallow the lump that was in my throat. I walked to through the backyard and into the field. I reached the field and walked to the other end of it. I stepped into the helicopter to see that Sandy was ready and waiting for me. He had been watching me make the journey across the field. *Wow,* I thought, *I forgot that I will always be watched, for my own protection until all of the Goldtrompers had been killed.*

"Are you ready to go?" He asked.

I adjusted my suit. "Yup. I'm all set." We buckled our seatbelts. The helicopter rose from off the ground. It flew towards the White House. We didn't talk the whole ride, because Sandy had fallen asleep. Finally after two hours of flying we reached the White House. The helicopter landed on the roof, and I grabbed my suit and the PadPad. Sandy and I stepped off of the helicopter. He led me to a trap door which he opened. He stepped down the stairs that were under the trap door. "Follow me, Jackson."

I followed Sandy down the stairs. We came to a hallway were many doors lined the sides. You can stay in this room

Jackson." I looked around the room. There was a king sized bed and a dresser. It looked really cozy. I threw my suit into the room and gently put my PadPad onto the dresser. I walked back out of the room and ran to catch up to Sandy who had already walked to the end of the hallway. "I will bring you to the conference room where the United Nations members are meeting. Since you were gone, all the nations of the world have joined in this committee. There are about one thousand members." We walked onto a platform which faced hundreds of seats where hundreds of men were sitting. I went up to the stand. "Supreme members of the United Nations, have you decided to listen to me?"

One of the men rose. "I am Gordon Flemin. I am the spokesperson for the United Nations. Yesterday Sandy was wearing a camera in which we saw what type of person you were. We have decided to listen to everything that you say for the next month. Now tell us how you think we can kill the creatures." The man sat back down in his chair.

"Well," I began. "The creatures are really called Goldtrompers. I met the first Goldtromper when I was on the Padmins' planet. If you put a spacesuit on then the Goldtrompers can't bite you. There is a new gun that I have discovered on one of the planets that I visited. Here are the plans." I had memorized the plans for the huli, which is the gun used by the Hopgulies. I watched as all the UN members wrote down the plans that I recited from memory. Each member had a carrier. The UN members handed the plans to the carriers, and the carriers rushed off.

Gordon Flemin stood up. "We have just sent the plans to the manufacturing plant in our capital cities. They will produce samples, test them, and then produce them. By tomorrow the world will have at least a million of those guns."

"But there is a problem," I interrupted. "The guns have special bullets that are made out of crushed copper mixed with gold ore."

The UN members frowned and whispered something into the ears of their second carrier. Gordon Flemin was still standing, "We have just sent messages to every country in the world telling them to give their gold and copper to the government. Unfortunately there is a really rich tycoon in Florida, Mr. Timret, who has most of the gold in the world. He won't give us his gold so, we'll have to take it from him. I will send 100 Navy Penguins to attack today. You can go along. Do you agree?"

"Yes," I replied. Navy Penguins are the modern day Navy Seals. They all carry lightweight bazookas with J-16s - extremely powerful guns. "Can I have a pill that makes me not have to eat for a week, please?" I asked.

"Sure," replied Mr. Flemin as he arose once more. "I'll put it in your room." Mr. Flemin must be a very fit man because he continually had to sit and stand.

I walked off of the platform and went back to my room. I put on my suit which still had the huli strapped to it and ate the pill that would allow me to not have to eat. I walked back to the helicopter and climbed aboard. Sandy was already there. "We need to go to Mr. Timret's house," I instructed.

The helicopter rose off of the ground and started flying towards the setting sun. Sandy stretched his hands. "I was

95

wondering when the UN would finally take the gold from Mr. Timret. Mr. Timret has lately been smuggling gold out of this country for years now. They just recently were able to prove it and not it is time to make things right."

"The pilot put on boost activation, so we will arrive in Florida in two hours. Get some sleep," commanded Sandy.

I fell asleep after about five minutes to the sound of the helicopters blades whirling through the air. I awoke to see Sandy standing over me and gently tapping me with his foot. "Wake up, sleepy head. The Navy Penguins will be here soon. You need to scout out the area so you can attack it. Mr. Timret has about one hundred thugs that he keeps for hurting people." It was nice that we were still circling the house so I could get an aerial view of it. The house had a huge wall around is. I noticed that there was a shed that was about three feet wide and three feet long. It was outside of the walls which were made out of the same material as the house. A man walked into the shed. "Tell the Navy Penguins to land by that shed," I told Sandy, who was standing and looking out of the windows on the sides of the helicopter. He radioed the new information to the captain of the Navy Penguins. We landed by the shed and Sandy and I stepped out. Just as we stepped out the Navy Penguin helicopters appeared above our heads. The helicopters landed next to Sandy's helicopter and many men stepped out. One of the Navy Penguins walked over to me and held out his hand. "I'm Jeff McKoy, you must be Jackson Williams. It's mice to meet you."

I shook Jeff's hand. "You can call me Jackson."

"And you can call me Jeff."

"Ok," I laughed. "So here's the plan. I think that shed has an underground entrance to the house. I saw a man go into the shed. He hasn't come out for about ten minutes."

"Ok, I'll tell my men to go into the shed." Jeff walked over to his men and shared the information, "Go into the shed. We think there is a secret passageway that leads to the house. Be careful. Mr. Timret is a really crazy man." All the men started walking towards the shed in a line. Two of the men kicked opened the door and then jumped back. Nothing came out so the men crept into the shed. Sure enough, in the far left corner was a dark hole with a ladder descending down into the abyss. I was the eighth person from the front. I followed the Navy Penguins in single file up the tunnel. About a half a mile down a dimly lit passageway we came to a door. The first Navy Penguin took his bazooka and blasted the door down. We rushed into the room to see piles of gold lining the walls. Suddenly a door on the other side of the room was thrown open and tons of guys came streaming into the room. A huge fight occurred in the small room. I unstrapped my huli and blasted away. My huli did more damage than the J-16s did. When I noticed that out enemy was no longer standing I hollered, "Stop shooting."

Everyone stopped shooting. As soon as the smoke cleared I looked around the room. Five Navy Penguins were dead, but we had killed all of the thugs. "Take all the gold and bring it to the helicopters," I ordered. The men did as they were told. After all the gold had been cleared away we walked back down the passageway. We blasted down the wall of the shed and then ran towards the house. "Destroy the house," I hollered. The men started blasting the house with their bazookas. A man came running out of the house. Jeff grabbed him and brought him to me. "This is Mr. Timret," Jeff said. "Should I tie him up and put him with the gold."

I nodded. The house was in ruins so I walked back to the helicopters and stepped into Sandy's helicopter. All the men stepped into their helicopters and we flew away. We arrived back at the White House at 6:00 P.M. I went straight to my room. I was so tired that I went to sleep.

Chapter 12

The next morning I awoke and stepped out of bed. I heard a knock, so I opened my door. "Hi," greeted Sandy. "Everyone is waiting for you to get up. Everything is ready. Last night we made all the ammunition for those guns."

"Yikes," I exclaimed. I quickly got dressed and put my suit in a backpack which I had found in the closet. I ran up to the helicopter on the roof of the White House and stepped inside. As soon as I was seated, the helicopter rose into the air. It started flying away from the White House. "We are going to meet all the UN fighters at the Washington D.C. Airport," Sandy said. After flying for two minutes we arrived on the roof of the airport. We walked to a trap door in the roof. The trap door had a ladder which went down into a passageway. We walked down the passageway until we came into a huge room where there were at least five thousand soldiers who each had a huli in their hand. "Hello everyone," I shouted. "Sorry for being so late. Everyone board the planes." The men started walking towards six doors that were along the wall. I boarded last to make sure that no one was left behind. I walked through the door which read 5 onto a little ramp that led into the plane. The first class seats were already mostly full with soldiers so I went to the back and sat down next to one of the men.

"What's your name?" I asked.

"I'm Arman Soman Oman. I am from Saudi Arabia. I like the US though. Everything is way bigger, even the people. What's your name?" he asked.

"My name is Jackson Williams," I replied.

"Oh," Arman interrupted. "You're the guy that got lost in space, so you're our captain."

"Yup."

"Wow, why didn't you sit in the first class seats?"

"Well," I answered. "I don't really need such nice seats. These seats are fine for me."

"But didn't you hear that there was a special seat saved for you on plane 1?"

"No, I didn't." I yawned. "I'm sorry, I think the time change from the invisible planet back to earth has really messed me up. Do you mind if I go to sleep? I'm really tired."

"Sure, go right ahead. We will arrive in Hawaii in about eight hours," Arman told me.

I fell asleep in less than five minutes. I started dreaming about the Hopgulies. They were having a debate on who should be the next governor. They were all shouting over each other. *When will the Hopgulies ever learn to not interrupt each other,* I thought in my sleep. I must have started laughing in my sleep because when I started waking up I could hear Arman asking why I was laughing.

"Oh, I just remembered something," I replied.

"Well, we are about to land in Hawaii."

Just then I heard a voice from the speaker which was above my head. "We are landing in the Honolulu Airport in five minutes. Please fasten your seat belts. Thank you for choosing The White House Airline, even though you didn't have a choice.

We hope you have wonderful day." I popped my seatbelt back on and looked out the window. I could see the coast of the island. The ocean looked like a mass of blue that expanded forever. The land looked like a quilt that had doll houses on it. The banana farms made the trees give off a yellow radiance. A city rose up in the distance. Skyscrapers towered towards the sky. As we reached the airport, I could faintly see people scurrying around in the city. My ears started to pop, so I laid back and tried to yawn. The plane jolted as it landed, then slowly decelerated until it stopped near the airport. An escalator on wheels was pushed to the door of the plane. The men and I walked off of the plane and went into the airport. All the men gathered around me so I started to speak, "If we kill the original Goldtromper then all the other Goldtrompers will go back to who they originally were. Our first job is to find him. Let's go scout the city in groups of twenty. We walked back out of the airport and started walking through the city. Some of the men followed me around the city. Suddenly, twenty Goldtrompers appeared in front of us. The Goldtrompers were about twelve feet tall. I took out my huli and started shooting the Goldtrompers. In the meantime 5 of the UN Fighters were eaten. The Goldtromper that ate the UN Fighter would then spit it out and a new Goldtromper would appear for every UN Fighter that they ate. We blasted away with our hulis until every Goldtromper was dead. I hoped we would get the original Goldtromper soon, so that our UN friends would come back to life. As we continued down the street, all of a sudden eighty Goldtrompers flew above our heads and started spiting huge gold blobs onto our heads. If a golden blob hit your head then you turned into a Goldtromper.

The soldiers and I ran to hide in the nearby buildings. What we did was a huge mistake. If a golden blob hit a building then that building would become a Goldtromper. Sadly one of the fifty foot tall buildings was hit and a huge Goldtromper arose from the ground. We had managed to kill all of the flying Goldtrompers so we focused our fire on the huge Goldtromper. My ammunition clip was empty so I took a magazine from out of my backpack. The Goldtromper was eating men left and right. I raised my gun and shot it in the mouth. It roared and threw back its head. It had no eyes, ears, hair, or nose. The heads of all the Goldtrompers were just one big mouth. This extra-large one died after the bullet went its mouth and then turned back into the building that it had been before. The Goldtrompers were indeed strange creatures. When the Goldtromper fell all the men that it had eaten climbed out. I don't think the big Goldtrompers could back anymore Goldtrompers. At least four hundred UN Fighters had become Goldtrompers so we had to kill them. We all felt bad about killing our own men, but we felt better that they would be revived once the original Goldtromper was dead.

We started walking towards the Goldtrompers' hideout. Suddenly, a giant foot stepped onto the group of soldiers. Two hundred of us died. I gasped and looked up. There was a Goldtromper that was so tall that I could hardly see its head. It was crushing tons of our men. "Follow me!" I shouted.

All the remaining men started running towards me. I sprinted towards the base. Suddenly, a group of flying Goldtrompers flew overhead and started spitting blobs. Hundreds of the UN Fighters were becoming Goldtrompers. Now, only forty soldiers and I were left. Was there any hope or were we goners? We ran into the Goldtrompers base. There was a building so we ran into it. Suddenly, I saw a Goldtromper coming towards us so I ran down a ladder that led into the earth. When I reached the bottom I saw that we were in a huge room. I heard footsteps approaching so we ran through a door that was to our left. It turns out that it was a bathroom. We heard things talking beneath us. One of the men found a piece of floorboard that could be lifted. Suddenly we heard something say, "They're in here." My heart skipped a beat. The soldiers and I started panicking. We rushed towards the tile and dove into the light. *Wait,* I thought. *Why is it light?* We fell for about ten minutes until we reached the bottom. Miraculously we didn't fall onto each other. The men and I stood up. The light was really intense. We had to shield our eyes because the light was so bright. As our eyes adjusted to the light I realized that we were in a different world. Apparently we had fallen through a warp hole.

Chapter 13

Suddenly, a hoard of dwarf's came running towards us. We turned around and ran the other way. I saw a giant stone tower in the distance. The UN Fighters and I ran towards the building. The building was about a mile away in a field. I looked back. The dwarves had stopped chasing us. I slowed down to catch my breath. Along the edge of the field there was a forest of pine trees. In front of the forest there was a river. The grass was about a foot tall. As soon as we reached the tower a group of centaurs came running out of the woods and across the river. The centaurs looked exactly like the centaurs in fairy tales. The centaurs had the body of a horse. Instead of a horse head the centaur had the body of a man from the waist up.

The centaurs were shouting and screaming and shooting arrows at us. We ran into the tower and shut the door. As soon as the door was closed the centaurs arrived and were pounding on the door. The door was knocked down and they galloped in. The soldiers and I started blasting the centaurs with our huli guns. The centaurs killed five men before they all died. The remaining thirty-five men and I walked back out of the tower and towards some mountains that were in the distance. On the way to the mountain a group of about one hundred dwarves appeared on the brow of the hill. They were standing in a line on the top of the hill. This made us run even faster toward the mountain. We came upon a group of elves who were sitting under a tree. The elves had big pointy ears. They had flowing brown hair. *They look just like the elves in The Lord of the Rings,* I thought. The Lord of the Rings was a video that I had watched when I was about twelve. It had just come out and I bought it. The elves that I saw now had much bigger ears than the elves in the Lord of the Rings. As we approached one of them asked, "Who are you, and what are you doing in the realm of his majesty, Fidulo the Wise?"

"We are humans, who are trying to get back to earth," I answered. "Do you know how to get back to earth?"

"Yes, I do," replied the elf, "I am Ilitimar. I will show you the way to exit this world. If you kill the Centaur king then we will kill the Goldtrompers' leader."

"How do you know about the Goldtrompers?" I asked suspiciously.

"Our ancestors are the stars and they whisper to us about all the things that go on in your world."

"Where are all the centaurs?" I asked.

"They live in the enchanted forest beyond the Great Tower. No one has dared venture into the depths of the enchanted forest, because no one ever returns. Some say that giant creatures live in the depths of those forests. Come with me. I will show you the way to the Centaur Castle. When you kill the Centaur king then a portal will appear above the dead king. Enter into that portal and you will see two thousand elves in front of you. Those elves will listen to everything that you say. As soon as the Goldtromper leader is dead those elves will disappear. Now follow me."

Wow! Maybe we had a better chance of winning with the elves on our side! The soldiers and I followed Ilitimar back towards the tower. As we walked towards the purple forest, I noticed that the birds in this world were huge. There was a bird that had a wingspan of about ten feet. Suddenly, a huge animal lumbered past us. Ilitimar lifted his bow and shot the creature.

"That was a Snorthog. They are like your warthogs except they are much bigger," Ilitimar broke the silence. I looked at the dead creature. It was as big as an elephant. It was all hairy and it looked scary. Ilitimar continued, "There's the path." Ilitimar pointed at a path that was about twenty yards away across the river. The elves stopped and the soldiers and I walked on. We crossed the shallow river and walked towards the path. We entered the path and walked for abut ten minutes. I glanced around. The trees were all purple. The branches on the trees were black. The ground was lime green. Suddenly a giant spider crawled across the path. "That must have been at least two feet tall," one of the men whispered.

"Why was I chosen to kill the Goldtromper?" one of the men complained.

"Ugh."

"Why did I even try out in the tournament to let us fight?" said another. I knew we had to get back to earth quickly, or all of the men's moral would drop drastically.

Suddenly a huge spider web crossed the path which blocked our view. I brushed the web aside and what I saw made me gasp. There in a clearing was a gigantic spider. Each of its eight legs was about five feet long. Its hairy body was huge. It scurried towards us and started attacking us with its legs. I lifted my huli and blasted away. I shot one of the creatures legs off which made the spider turn and rush towards me! Before I knew it the spider had wrapped my legs up in a sticky spider web. I tried escaping but the spiders big legs knocked my down.

I looked at the soldiers. They were shooting the spider, but the spider wasn't dying. The spider hadn't wrapped up my head so I shouted, "Shoot its eyes." One of the men shot the spider in the left eye and the spider started hissing. I unrolled myself as much as possible from the web and managed to get somewhat untangled. My men rushed over and unwrapped me the rest of the way.

After running for about ten minutes, we came upon a group of dwarves. They had huge beards that almost reached the ground. Each of the dwarves had a huge battle axe in their hands. We stopped to look at the sleeping dwarves. I felt a pair of rough hands grab me from behind. Something behind us shouted and the sleeping dwarves immediately woke up. Our captors tied our hands behind our backs. Some dwarves must have been hiding so they could come out of the woods to capture us. The dwarves pushed us down the path for about thirty minutes. My hands were very sore. None of the dwarves had talked at all during the last thirty minutes, but suddenly one of the dwarves spoke. "Everyone halt." Everyone stopped. The dwarf continued, "I am Trumpket the dwarf. What are you doing in the forests of the High King Umnet the Dwarf?"

"We are travelers from the world above and we are trying to kill the Centaur king. The elf Ilitimar told us that if we kill the Centaur king then the elves would come to our world and kill my enemies."

"Did you here that, men?! He is going to kill the Centaur king!" shouted Trumpket.

The men started shouting, "Huzzah!"

"Hurray for the human!"

"Can you show us how you weapons work?" asked one of the dwarves, who looked to be about 700 years old with hair as white as snow down to his waist.

"Sure," I replied. I lifted my gun and shot a tree that was about ten yards away. A bright light flooded out of my huli. The bullet made a huge hole in the tree. The tree started cracking and the huge gnarly tree fell to the ground. All the dwarves' jaws dropped. Their eyes were as big as saucer. "Well," began Trumpket, "You won't have any problem in defeating the Centaur king, then. Follow this path. Make sure that you don't leave the path."

We walked back down the path until we got to a huge mountain. We climbed the mountain until there was a fork in the pathway. One path led through a door into the heart of the mountain. The other path looked like it led around the mountain. On the path through the mountain there was a sign which had many different languages on it. My eyes scrolled down to human. There was some writing which read, "Short Cut to the Centaur Castle." Well, I needed to get home as soon as possible, but the dwarf told us not to go off of the path. Maybe this was the path. It seemed to be the path. I decided that we would go through the mountain. The soldiers and I walked up the path and through the doors. As soon as we walked through the doors they shut. As our eyes adjusted to the darkness my heart was telling me to go back. I didn't feel comfortable about this passageway. There was no turning back so we walked on. We came to a door which I shot down with my huli. Suddenly a weird odor filled the room. I watched as my comrades all fainted. I managed to drag myself back to the double doors that led out of the mountain. Then I fainted.

When I came to, the odor was gone. I stretched my stiffened muscles and walked down the passage way. The door was open and I saw that the soldiers were gone. I saw horse prints in the soil so I decided to follow them. The prints went down the passage way and into another passage way. The prints walked down another passage way that had a light at the end of it. I went to that light. It was the open air. I was relieved. I climbed out of the passageway and out into the open air. I was on the top of a mountain. I looked into the valley and saw a huge castle. Its topmost towers scraped the sky. I ran down the path that led to the castle. I reached the castle just as the sun was setting behind it. I pushed aside some foliage and stepped into the clearing that the castle was in. The castle had a feeling a magic about it. The stone walls of the castle were covered in vines. I walked towards the entrance. Suddenly, hands grabbed my arms again! I was lifted into the air and raced through the castle. I looked at the scenery as I rushed by. I was carried past a kitchen with a beautiful aroma of baking which filled my nostrils. I was rushed past a huge dungeon were the aroma of baking was replaced by the stench of rotting bodies.

I was carried up at least ten flights of stairs. Finally I was brought to a huge great hall. The great hall's ceiling must have been twenty feet tall. There was a long purple carpet that stretched in the center of the room from one end to the other. Directly across from me there was a platform where a centaur with a crown was standing. On either side of the rug hundreds of centaurs were standing. The centaur with the crown spoke, "Hello human. What are you doing in the realm of Hefrop the Great?"

I bowed low, "I have come to trade, noble sir."

"What do you want to trade?" the king asked.

"I will trade my companions for this gun. Only you can touch it. No one but Hefrop the Great may touch this sacred weapon."

"What can it do? Can it kill anybody?"

"I lifted the huli above my head. "Yes, it can easily kill anyone."

"Bring his companions," the king ordered one of the centaurs who were standing nearby. In less than five minutes all of my soldiers were there.

"Give me the gun!" the king shouted.

"You have to come get it. It is too powerful for me to bring up to your majesty."

"I will send someone to get it then," Hefrop the Great declared.

"No," I replied. "That person will take it from me and shoot you with it. You must come get the gun yourself."

The centaur king slowly trotted over to me. He stood in front of me and held out his hand. I lifted the gun and shot him. Instantly a portal appeared and the soldiers and I rushed forward. As soon as we stepped into the portal we appeared on one of the beaches of Honolulu. In front of us were two thousand elf warriors who were hollering and waving their bows.

"Everyone attack those beasts!" I shouted over the ruckus. All the elves rushed forward and started attacking the

Goldtrompers. The elves climbed up the sides of the big Goldtrompers and climbed into their mouths. Then the elf would start shooting arrows into the throat of the Goldtromper. The Goldtromper would fall and the elf would climb out of the mouth of the Goldtromper and attack the next one. "Follow me!" I shouted to a group of two hundred elves. I ran towards the Goldtromper base. Suddenly, I saw a twelve foot tall Goldtromper and I realized that it was the original Goldtromper. It recognized me, because it rushed forward and started throwing fire and ice at me. The thought suddenly came to me; He must have eaten some Padmin. That is why he can throw fire, ice, and rock at us, I thought. And for that he must die! The elves rushed onto the Goldtromper and started slashing the Goldtromper with their daggers. The Goldtromper was throwing the elves off and throwing rock, ice, and fire at them. Finally one of the elves managed to get into the Goldtromper's mouth. The Goldtromper gave a huge roar and lay still. Cheers went up from my men.

Instantly, all the Goldtrompers became humans and all the elves disappeared. All of the dead Goldtompers, except the original who must have been a Goldtromper for too long to be able to turn back into a human, turned back into their human forms. Hawaii and the world were saved from the terror of the Goldtromper.

The thirty-five soldiers and I walked back to the airport and boarded one of the five planes that were waiting for us. It was only 7:00 P.M., 1 hour since our victory. I saw on the airplane news channel that our success was already being shown to the world. I smiled as I thought of my family and Makayla getting the good news! I imagined their relief and joy.

The planes took off and we headed towards Washington D.C. We arrived at 11:00 P.M. I went up to the roof of the airport and boarded the helicopter. Sandy was waiting for me in the cockpit. As soon as we landed at the White House I went to my room and fell into bed, exhausted. What a long day!

Chapter 14

The next morning I woke up and the first thing I did was text Makayla and my family to let them know that I was coming home as soon as possible. I then looked to my nightstand and found a message which read, "Come to the UN meeting room." I walked to the UN meeting room and arrived just as the last UN member sat down. I walked up to the podium. "I have defeated the Goldtrompers with the help of the uhhhh...... soldiers."

Even though the UN Leaders had heard the news, they all cheered. They then stood up and started clapping their hands to officially acknowledge us. They sat back down and Mr. Flemin stayed standing. "We have decided to ask for your advice in how to rebuild the towns and cities that the Goldtrompers destroyed."

"I would advise you to each choose one city that your own country will help. The bigger cities could be helped by the bigger countries. The smaller countries can help the smaller cities. If each country helps one city then the work will be spread evenly around the world. We don't want just one country to help. We want to be the United Nations. Not the Untied Nations."

All the members nodded their heads. Mr. Flemin stood up again." I think that we all agree with you. Now everyone will stand up and say what city they are going to help."

The Chinese members stood up, "We will help Honolulu."

The United Kingdom members stood up, "We will help Manilla."

The Russian members rose from their seats, "We will help Taiwan."

All the members stood up and announced who their country would help. Finally everyone had finished speaking and the meeting was dismissed. I went back to my room where I met Sandy, who was waiting to escort me home.

I gathered my things and walked up to the helicopter, which was on the roof of the White House. Sandy and I stepped inside and sat down. As soon as we were seated the helicopter rose into the air and flew towards my house.

After about 2 minutes of flying, I got impatient so I picked up the PadPad. I hit the call button. Suddenly I heard a voice, "Is it you human?"

"Hey, Gulpoy, is it really you?!" I excitedly hollered.

"Yes, Human. Since you have gone things have been getting back to normal. Aforot is ruling the Padmin very wisely. We have rebuilt the village and the creatures have stopped attacking us. We made a statue of you and put it next to the shouting rock. We are all very grateful and thankful."

I had tears in my eyes. Gulpoy went on, "You defeated the Goldtromper, right? Well, I'm proud of you. You are our hero human." The voice on the other end started going fuzzy and then stopped all together. Tears were slowly going down my face. Sandy was looking at me with a weird expression on his face. "I don't know who that was, but all I can say is that you sure had a crazy adventure somewhere."

I wiped the tears from my cheeks. "Yeah, it was quiet an adventure all right. First I defeated all the Padmins' enemies. Then creatures from another planet, the Hopgulies, came and carried me away. They made me defeat their enemies in order for me to go home. It was really wild. I ended up crashing a plane into the enemy's base which made the base explode. Then I spent four days in the hospital recovering from my wounds. The Hopgulies then sent me home, where I had to defeat the main Goldtromper. While I was hiding from the Goldtrompers, my soldiers and I fell into the underworld where I met an elf guy. The elf said that if I killed the centaur king then a portal would appear to bring my soldiers and I home. Also, if I killed the centaur king then two thousand elves would help me kill all the Goldtrompers. After killing a giant spider, I was carried off by some centaurs who brought me to the centaur king where I killed him. A portal appeared and my soldiers and I stepped into it. When we stepped through the portal two thousand elves were in front of me. We killed the original Goldtromper and the rest of them turned into humans again. The rest, as they say, is history."

By the time I was done the helicopter was already landing the field. I walked to the house. My family ran out to greet me again.

"Hi again, son," my dad said patting me on the back.

"Hi, Jackson," the rest of my family said not at all in unison.

"Hey guys," I replied.

We walked inside and life went back to normal. Makayla and I planned our weddings and enjoyed being together again. I was glad that I didn't have to fight or go anywhere. Now, I was free to live as I chose. I was happy to be home again.

Epilogue

10 years later, I am now married to Makayla. We have five kids and a house in Kalamazoo, Michigan. I was weeding in my garden when I came upon a Padplant.

THE END